WOLF MAN

JOHN REINHARD DIZON

CHAPTER ONE

Kane North was the biggest crack dealer in NYC, and no one in the NYPD, the DEA or the rival organizations in the Tri-State area expected his rise to taper off any time soon. He had cocaine coming in from the Florida Keys, the Mexican and Canadian borders, and dozens of points along the Northeast seacoast. It was being converted to crack in hundreds of underground labs in New York, New Jersey and Pennsylvania, and distributed from over a thousand crack houses throughout the area. It was estimated that the North Network was grossing over a million dollars a day before expenses, and North's only concern was the staggering burden it was placing on his money-laundering corporations.

Many of their biggest customers were people in the entertainment industry who had become addicted to cocaine, and were convinced that switching over to the crack pipe would give them greater energy and euphoria than ever. Getting hooked on crack made them slaves to the narcotic, and a large majority found their professional reputations ruined and their income dwindling so as not to be able to afford the quantity they were consuming. Females paid the highest price for their addictions, as many of them were forced to do sexual favors in exchange for what they could not buy.

Mirjana Dragana was one of these unfortunates. She was an aspiring model who had been given a chance at a starring role in a B-movie being produced by one of North's filmmaking tax writeoffs. She had been turned onto coke by the movie directors, and soon graduated to crack with their encouragement. The beautiful Serbian had put her modeling career on hold and was now entirely dependent on her earnings from the movie, production of which was suddenly postponed. She found herself unemployed and addicted to the product, and after spending her savings to satisfy her cravings, she was forced to meet with North himself to resolve her problem.

She had heard rumors of the depredations suffered by women who had been lured to North's suite in a penthouse bordering East Harlem in similar situations to her own. She had confided in a close friend, Steve Lurgan, who lived in the three-story apartment building in Soho she rented upon arriving in NYC. Lurgan was a photojournalist who had just returned from Eastern Europe and had covered the war in Bosnia in the 90's. He knew some Serbian and quickly made friends with Jana. He had watched her decline caused by drug abuse but would not compromise their friendship by criticizing her. It was only when she told him that she was meeting personally with North that he offered advice.

"Jana, please be careful when you go up there," Lurgan pleaded. "I read the papers and I've got connections. These people are involved in drugs, and I wouldn't put it past them to try and involve you in something immoral to tide you over until the movie production resumes."

"Don't worry, Steve," Jana assured him. She was an ash blonde with pale blue eyes, a smallish nose and thick lips, her natural beauty enhanced by an hourglass figure and a generous bosom. "I know you are my friend and you care for me. I will be fine, I know what I am doing. Most of these companies have insurance covering loss of income, and I believe they will be able to come up with enough to keep me on the payroll until they start filming again."

Despite her courageous veneer, she was filled with trepidation as she arrived at North's Lenox Avenue brownstone that evening. There were four gangsters standing outside the building, and they announced her arrival by cell phone before she was permitted entrance. Four more gangsters met her in the lobby, and they escorted her to the end of the hall where a heavy steel door was guarded by two pistol-packing gunmen.

"Hey, baby," a tall, slender black man was seated on a throne on a dais in a parlor area the size of a commercial showroom. She looked around the lavishly furnished area where six other blacks relaxed on the overstuffed sofas and chairs around the living room. They stared at her as if a piece of candy had walked into the room. "Let my boy get you a drink. Come on up here and tell me what I can do for you."

"I---I came to discuss my position with Player Productions," Jana came forward tentatively, walking to the edge of the platform before North beckoned her forth. She stepped up onto the dais and walked timidly over to where Kane sat. The man leered at her lustfully, his coke-flushed eyes glittering over his wide nostrils and Luciferian goatee.

"Girl, you can assume any position you like to get anything you want around here," North grinned as his henchmen cackled in amusement. "Now, I saw some of the outtakes from that flick you starring in, and there is no way that a woman who looks like you ain't gonna have no place in this organization."

"Thank you," Jana managed. "It's just that they stopped sending checks to the cast members and crew since the first of the month, and it is very difficult to make do with the production having been postponed. I don't know if you're aware that I canceled my modeling assignments to devote my full time to this project."

"Now, Jana---it is Jana, isn't it? I make it my business to know every detail of my various enterprises. I'm the kind of entrepreneur who likes to keep hands-on every-thing in his operation, you know what I'm saying?" North looked her over approvingly. "I know your story, baby, and I want to do everything in my power to get you right where you wanna be. Now, I know you were in the fast lane with my cruisers, and the producers liked you not only because of your talent, but your ability to interact behind the scenes. I know you were a real party girl, most oftentimes the life of the party. Now, I would feel like I got beat if I never once got to get some party time with you myself. My road dogs here pretty well feel the same way."

"Mr. North, sir," she lowered her eyes, realizing how they were all leering at her, "part of the reason why I am here is because I overextended my personal budget by over-socializing. I realize that I got caught up in the whole Broadway mentality, and wasted more money than I had a right to misappropriate. I have bills to pay, and have not anticipated the interruption of income. I misjudged the solvency of the company by assuming that since you were the owner, they would have the advantage of your solidity. All I ask is that I can get at least one more month of paychecks, which of course would be deducted from my earnings when the project is completed."

"Baby, I don't know how else to break it to you, but *Showdown In Serbia* has flatlined," North smirked. "Our marketing analysts have looked it over, and they don't see it going anywhere past Blockbuster. I got to pull the plug on this, pretty girl, but that don't necessarily mean I needs to pull the plug on you."

"Is there---are there---any other projects that I can get in on?" she managed.

"Well now, you know that most of your marketability is going to be predicated by your screen attraction," North leaned forward on his velvet and gold throne. "I personally haven't had a chance to check out your file. I'm sorry to say I don't have a clue as to what my studio is throwing down all this money for. Would I be out of place in asking if we can do a screen test here so I can decide whether to cut you a big check?"

"Why, no," Jana could not possibly refuse.

"I hope you won't mind removing your blouse, so I can see what you would look like in a bikini," Kane produced a bag of cocaine appearing as a baggie full of laundry detergent.

"Why...no," Jana swallowed hard. The room was silent as the grave before she hesitantly began unbuttoning her blouse.

"Now that is what I call charisma," Kane grinned as he appreciated her large breasts in their lace bra. "Why don't you take off them jeans so we can see what that bikini shot's really gonna sell? I think we can do up a couple lines here to get rid of some of that nervousness. You know, that's what we looking for, the kind of lady who just don't drop her drawers at the drop of a hat."

There was a scratching at the door, almost as if someone had let a dog into the hallway outside. Kane had disregarded it when he first heard it, but now it was a distraction without explanation. North pulled out his cell phone and hit the contact number but got no response.

"Look, somebody go outside and tell those mofos that they need to get on the ball," Kane cut the howling short as Jana allowed her jeans to drop to her ankles. "They be a million mofos wantin' to get in that hallway, and I payin' some big money to make sho' they ain't! Now get them dogs on that bone before I send them all back to the pound!"

The hulking gunman, standing at nearly seven foot tall and weighing over three hundred pounds, drew his Uzi as he lumbered towards the door and threw it open.

At once the carnage began.

Jana Dragana woke up in Bellevue Hospital the next morning and immediately went into a panic. Memories of the mayhem of the previous night flooded her mind, but the overriding fright was the fact that she had no way to pay for whatever medical costs she was incurring.

"What---what am I doing here!" she exclaimed as a nurse and a doctor were quick to record her responses on a clipboard. "I was brought here unawares, I have no money to pay for this!"

"It's okay, Ms. Dragana," the nurse assured her. "We're charging it to Mr. North's account with Player Productions, or possibly with one of his many other insurance accounts. If they deny the claim, you can be sure that the Hospital will provide you with a convenient and affordable payment plan."

"Ms. Dragana, are you currently enrolled in any detox

programs, or seeking treatment for narcotic dependence?" the doctor was hesitant. "The only reason I ask is because the paramedics had a great deal of difficulty placing you under sedation. Most of the time it is caused by a high tolerance to drugs which we are obliged to mention before your release."

"No, no, there is no problem," Jana's eyes darted about the room. "I wish to leave immediately. I ask that my clothing and personal property be returned at once."

"Of course, Ms. Dragana," the nurse replied as the doctor left the room. "You have a visitor who insists on seeing you, a Mr. Lurgan."

"Certainly," Jana managed as the nurse retrieved her clothes from a curtained closet. "Let him in."

Steve Lurgan came to her bedside as soon as the nurse permitted him entry. He was a muscular man of average height, packing 185 pounds onto a 5'9" frame. He had wavy jet black hair, piercing blue eyes and a strong jaw. He was ruggedly handsome and had always been seen favorably by Jana, who would have taken him on as a boyfriend if her aspirations and addictions had not complicated her life.

"Are you okay, Jana?" were his first words.

"I'm fine, they'll be releasing me shortly," she patted his hands as they held hers. "I'll be back at the apartment in an hour or so, we'll have coffee, okay?"

"Okay, buddy," he patted her hand before rising to leave. "See you at home."

Lurgan's mind was filled with apprehension as he walked down the hall towards the elevators that would take him to the grade level and the exit to First Avenue on Lower Manhattan. He was seriously infatuated with Jana, and had been agonized by her slow descent into crack addiction and her hellish association with North's organization. He knew that he had no right to meddle in her personal affairs, and any liberty he might take could justifiably result in the permanent loss of her friendship. He could only love her from a distance, and hope that perhaps one day his loyalty might lead to recognition and a bond somewhat more substantial.

"Mr. Lurgan?" he heard a familiar voice call from behind him. "Mr. Lurgan."

"Officer Lucic," Steve recognized him on sight. "How can I help?"

"Say, I really don't want to mess up your day," the blond, muscular officer ambled up to him, "but I was hoping you could spare a couple of minutes of your time. Do you think we could walk over to Starbucks?"

"You probably know my friend Jana's being released in a little while. I told her I'd meet her back at the apartment. Do you think we could do this at a better time?"

"I could take you downtown if I had to. Look, forget about Starbucks. You probably know I've been looking at you for a while. How did Jana Dragona get involved in your business?"

"My business," Steve walked over by the curb where the car Lucic was leaning on was parked. "I wish you would explain to me exactly what you think is my business."

"Come on, Steve," Darko Lucic shook his head, gazing at the azure sky above the Manhattan skyline. "I've got you at two of three recent homicides where the victims were killed under the same *modus operandi*. You know who let the dogs out, and you've got to tell me. If this goes beyond my control, who knows where this ends up? With all this terrorist bullshit going on these days, you might end up in Guantanamo or some other dirty place."

"Dogs," Steve threw his hands out in bemusement. "Officer Lucic---"

"Darko."

"Okay, Darko. What are you trying to pin on me? I don't own a dog, I never have. I don't know the first thing about dogs, I live in an apartment."

"Come on, Steve," Lucic massaged his temples. "You make it easy for me, I make it easy for you. I got drug dealers getting torn up by some attack dog three times since the beginning of last year. It just happens to be around the time you came back to New York after your return from Eastern Europe. The first incident went just fine, no slipups. The second time, you get made my one of my junkie rats walking away from the scene of the crime. Third time you get spotted again, I bring you some heat and you blow me off. Now here we are. Now I got motive, this girl you'd like to screw is getting pressured by Kane North to do the dirty for him and his buddies. They get ripped apart by an attack dog, and here we are with you visiting the sole survivor of the massacre. You're a war correspondent, Steve. Turn it around for a minute. If you were me, what are you looking at?"

"How do I know, Darko? You want me to do your job for you? I'm not a dog handler. Maybe someone's out there making moves against drug dealers and siccing dogs on them. Maybe I happened to be in the wrong place at the wrong time. You do what you think you got to do, but, at the risk of being punnish, you're barking up the wrong tree."

"Okay, you wanna play hardball. Your friend Jana is a crack addict. You can go running to her and she can call a HIPPA violation, but then you and I go to the mat and you gotta lose. I go back against her and you know she'll slip and fall somewhere. Look, we can't have vigilantes running loose siccing dogs on drug lords, regardless of how lofty your goal. You did some hard time in Bosnia, you know how the game is played. Maybe you came back here and thought you could apply your skills on the streets of New York. Not happening, Mr. Lurgan. I'm from Serbia, my relatives suffered and died during the conflict. I have seen what happens when people take the law into their own hands, and I will not stand by and see it happen here."

"I agree with you, Darko. I'm behind that one hundred percent."

"I got wolf hairs at the scene of the crimes, Lurgan," Lucic snarled in his face. "I got zoologists verifying that the bite marks on the victims were wolf bites. Somebody you know has trained wolves tearing drug dealers apart at these murder scenes. Look, I don't have any more sympathy for dealers than you do, especially ones who are ruining the lives of women like Jana Dragona. Still, there is a law that governs this nation, a law that protects and defends our people, a law that we cannot suspend at our discretion. I am sworn to uphold that law, and that law does not provide for vigilantes siccing wolves on drug dealers. You need to tell me who's behind this so I can make sure it doesn't happen again."

"What I can tell you is that I care very much about Jana," Lurgan insisted. "I don't need you to tell her that, I only hope you can appreciate it. I don't know anything about what you and your people came up with about where I was when you said I was. I'm a walker, I take long walks at night, it's just who I am. There's no law against people walking around town, is there? If I tried to tell you where I walk and when I walk, you'd probably try and have me sent to Bellevue."

"Been there done that," Lucic allowed. "I'm trying to

factor that in, but this last one is too hard to overlook. Think about this: if North's confederates find out that he and his bodyguards got dogged by someone, and they think for one minute that Jana had something to do with it, what do you think happens next?"

"It's not happening," Steve was adamant. "It's never gonna happen."

"Look, we can put you both into witness protection. We got plenty of choices. Tell me who's got the wolf and we can wrap this up. If they haven't killed any civilians, we may be able to give them a get-out-of-town option. *You* don't have plenty of choices. It happens again, and I drop a ton of weight on your girlfriend. I use her to get to you, and I don't give a crap if you tell her what I said. I'll put a thousand eyes on her, and when she snorts her next line we take her to MCC. She can't handle Metro, and she'll break apart because of you."

"You're all wrong, Darko," Steve insisted. 'I'll stay home and watch TV next month, you can stuff your wolves up your ass. You're scratching for leads and you don't have shit. I saw it in Bosnia, when they don't have anything they make something. I won't give you anything. You put your rats right on my porch, I don't give you shit."

"Yeah, so how're your boys gonna make it happen?" Darko called after him as he headed for the subway. "You gonna turn into a wolf?"

Steve walked away wordlessly, the safety and security of Jana Dragona as an overwhelming concern pounding in his head.

CHAPTER TWO

The nightmare began for Steve Lurgan in Kosovo around 1999. He had been investigating rumors around the Sar Mountains along the Albanian border where it was reported that KLA troops had brought Serbian citizens to slaughter. Even more horrific rumors circulated that the KLA had secret laboratories situated along the mountain range where Serbians were being butchered for their organs and body parts.

Steve was born in Queens, New York but had traveled back and forth from Ireland throughout his life to spend summers with his grandparents. He developed a love for travel and had been taken to the Continent by his relatives over the years. By the time he graduated from the University of Dublin with a degree in journalism, he had seen almost all the major cities in Western Europe. He had a yearning to see the rest of the continent, and took a job as a photojournalist to realize his dream. Only when the war broke out in Serbia in the 90's, he found that he could make more money selling his pictures to the highest bidder than tying himself down to one publisher. He decided to go free-lance, and it gave him more freedom than ever.

The Serbian War seemed to reflect the Troubles in Northern Ireland multiplied many times over. Racial and religious tensions had simmered in the region for centuries since the dynasty of the Ottoman Turks, cooling off sporadically only to boil over anew. Christians had struggled to find their place along the mountainous regions along the Balkan Peninsula, and as they grew with the support of fellow Christians in Western Europe, the Muslims found themselves on the low end of the economic scale. The ancient Illyrians gave way to the 6th century Slavs, followed by the Albanians in the 8th century and the Bulgarians in the 9th century. The Serbians had taken control over Kosovo until they were ousted by the Ottomans in 1389, and the Turks ruled the area until 1913 when it was re-occupied by Serbia.

In 1918, Kosovo became part of the Yugoslavian Federation, and the region was tossed about by the winds of war up to the present day. Steve had spent the entire 90's decade in Serbia and fell in love with the land and its people. It was during the time of the Grunge Revolution in the USA, and he delighted in bringing the new sound to the Serbian teens. Nirvana, Pearl Jam and REM were among their favorites, and Steve loved the fact that Serbian Army troops were kicking out the jams in their armored trucks as they patrolled the picturesque countryside.

Steve's first recollection of the rumors began at a Serbian restaurant in Kosovo where he was having lunch with Gunter Schenck of Reuters and Karen Jones from Associated Press. They saw four grim-faced Chinese men in black strutting in like gangsters, eyeing the other patrons balefully before walking to the bar and ordering drinks.

"Those guys are bad news, Steve," Gunter warned him. "Those are the kind of guys you want to forget you ever saw. Kinda like drug lords in Colombia, kings of the earth."

"Yeah, but we're in Kosovo," Steve continued looking over until they made eye contact, then he smiled and looked back at Gunter and Karen. "Long way from China."

"Problem is, they're dealing in the black market with the Kosovo Liberation Army," Gunter explained. "You've heard about the Chinese harvesting body organs for transplant operations? Well, these guys are spare parts dealers, if you know what I mean."

"You gotta be kidding me!" Steve exclaimed. "You mean, you're sitting here telling me this and you aren't out trying to score a Pulitzer on it? Hell, I've been here almost ten years and haven't heard a thing about it."

"That's because I like covering news stories in Kosovo, eating exotic food, drinking fine wine, having lunch with beautiful correspondents, and living and breathing in particular," Gunter winked at Karen. "Tracking down psychopaths in the Sar Mountains would be just as suicidal as hunting down drug dealers in the Amazon. Even the best of us know where to draw the line."

"This isn't the Amazon, Gunter," Steve sipped his *raki*. "There's lots of people living up in those mountains whose ancestors have lived there for centuries. One thing I've learned about Europe is that, basically, the common folk are the same everywhere. They're good people who don't mind helping travelers. I don't think it'd hurt for us to drive up and have a look around. If they have any reason to be scared or secretive, then you've got a story right there that opens up doors for more people to inquire about."

"You know, he's right," Karen, a lovely blue-eyed brunette, agreed. "It's disgusting to think someone would be taking advantage of a war zone like that. The United Nations has people all over the country, and they should know if there's something like this that needs looking into. I think we should go up and take a look. They've got most of the entry points into Bosnia blocked off right now, we're just sitting around cooling our heels anyway."

"You can't argue with a beautiful woman, everyone knows that," Gunter, a rugged blond German from Hannover, chuckled as he took a bite of his *sudzuk*. "All right, then let's finish up here and take the scenic tour. Just remember, if we see anything that remotely resembles armed troops, we're out of there quicker than you can say organ donor."

They finished their meal and decided to cruise up to Gusinje on the border of Montenegro. It was a rustic little town at the foot of the Accursed Mountains, and did not get many tourists or outsiders due to its remote location. They saw a shepherd tending to a flock of goats not far from the city limits along a spring and pulled over for a chat. The man spoke Serbian as did the three foreigners.

"You are far better limiting your visit to the town," the old man advised them. "They don't call that range the Prokletije for nothing. Tradition has it that it was created by the Devil himself. There is nothing but glaciers and limestone mazes in there, along with wolves and other dangerous animals. If you get lost and cannot find your way by nightfall, you may never return. There is a demon wolf in those mountains that has developed a taste for human blood. He only comes out at night when he knows he cannot be captured. Even the rebels fear him."

"So you know that the Kosovo Liberation Army is up in those mountains," Gunter pressed. "Have you heard rumors of them taking hostages and holding them captive up there?"

"It would make no sense," the old man replied. "Why would someone take hostages into an area where they could not even defend themselves?"

The journalists took leave of the old man and began in the general direction of Gusinje before Gunter veered off towards a steep mountain road.

"Okay, guys," Gunter decided, "I think we're about to bag the big one. If we can find traces of the KLA up here, we can tie in the local superstition to the rumors of the organ black-marketing and get enough of a human interest hook to put our names on this map. I say we drive up and take a look around. If we see anything that remotely looks like a military unit's been around here, Steve takes a pic and me and Karen'll do the rest."

They drove up the hill and found themselves upon a crest overlooking a canopied valley accessible only along a rocky path that wound through a limestone-strewn ravine. There was water running from the glaciers that caused silvery rivulets to spread across the trail. Gunter eased his jeep to a halt, concerned as to where this unmarked road might lead.

"I don't know, maybe we should get out and take a look," he decided.

He parked the truck and they began wandering along the limestone trail. Unknown to them, the old man was a lookout for KLA rebels whose base was located in the area. He cell phoned the guerrillas as soon as the reporters drove off, and they were alerted throughout the vicinity in turn. When the three journalists reached halfway down the ravine, they found themselves surrounded by riflemen who appeared along rock ledges on all sides.

"Hands in the air! You are surrounded!" a man called out in an Albanian accent.

"We're journalists, don't shoot!" Gunter cried as they did as they were told. "We came over here from Kosovo. We were investigating rumors of a giant wolf in the area."

"We think you have come here for something entirely different," the leader stepped forth, his AK-47 pointed at them. "Perhaps we can help you find what you are looking for."

"I left the keys in the jeep," Gunter muttered to the others. "If we make a break for it, one of us can get back to town and call the police. General Mladic's Serbian Army units are stationed just outside Kosovo. If they find out these guys are out here they'll come up with everything they have."

"We can't!" Steve insisted. "If they start shooting they might hit Karen!"

"Okay, Karen, you stay here and we'll run for help!" Gunter was ready and set.

"Bullshit!" she hissed. "You're not leaving me here to get chopped up for some organ market!"

"Run!" Gunter exclaimed.

They turned and made a mad dash back up the hill, and were both astonished and terrified by the sound of automatic fire behind them. Steve felt a searing pain in his left tricep followed by a burning impact against his right shoulder before a jolt to his right thigh sent him sprawling to the rocky ground. Dazedly he looked around and saw Karen to his left and Gunter to his right. They were lying face down and did not move.

"The one in the middle is still moving," the leader called out in Albanian. "Bring him with us. Go get their vehicle and throw the other two inside, drive it back to the base."

The pain was blazing by now, and Steve cried out involuntarily as they grabbed him underneath each arm and began dragging him. He hobbled along as best he could as a dozen of them converged upon the limestone trail ahead, and he was pulled into the middle of the group as they made their way deeper into the ravine.

"The journalists they send into this country are as reckless as they are stupid," the leader proclaimed to his comrades. "We set people in place with instructions to discourage these fools from rushing in to their doom, yet they insist on going to the exact place where they are told not to go! Even the legends of demons cannot dissuade them from going off to their death. All we can do is use their cameras to take pictures that they will never develop, and send them to publishers who will never hear from these poor fools again!"

Steve's mind was racing as he thought of how to escape this trap and send word to General Mladic's forces near Kosovo. He knew he was wounded but felt as if he could at least make it back to Gusinje if he could only get away. He knew once they got him back to their base, it was all over. They shot down the three of them without even trying to catch them. They were doubtlessly going to murder Steve as well, and there was a distinct possibility that they would be taking him somewhere to cut his vital organs out of his body to sell to the Chinese gangsters in Kosovo. Things seemed hopeless as they approached the cavern just ahead.

He felt dizzy from the loss of blood and did not feel as if he was going to be able to go much farther. He was about to speak out when he could hear them yelling and shouting around him. He thought they were heckling him, but realized there were popping and snapping sounds as tree limbs breaking along the sides of the ravine. The two men dragging him released him so that he fell to the ground, and he covered his head as best he could as a firefight raged around him. He heard men screaming and dying, but it seemed to end as suddenly as it began as the ambushers scurried down from the rocks.

"This one's fairly well shot up," one of the riflemen called back to the others after rolling Steve over. "He was bleeding before we got here."

"There's a couple of bodies in the jeep we intercepted," he heard another voice calling in Serbian from the other side of the hill. "There's also some camera equipment."

"Check his pockets," the leader came down from the hill overlooking the ravine. "He must be a reporter who came here with the other two."

The rifleman standing near Steve went through his pockets and handed his wallet to the leader. The man impassively glanced through its contents before approaching.

"I am Captain Evilenko," he introduced himself as Steve was pulled into a sitting position. "I have been assigned to hunt down the KLA company protecting this area. We suspected that they had enlisted the local farmers and shepherds as lookouts. That is why they have been able to avoid us all this time. When these men fail to report, the main unit will know they were intercepted. We will have to set up camp here and wait for them to move against us."

"Come," a sergeant came forth. "We will help dress your wounds and give you food and water."

"What---what of my friends?"

"We are a field unit, we cannot abandon this sector," Evilenko replied curtly. "Unfortunately we will have to bury your friends here so that wild animals do not get to them. If we were to send men back to the village, they would be reported to the enemy just as you were."

Steve watched as the soldiers began dropping their backpacks and setting them around the ravine while others dragged the dead KLA men into the cavern. Riflemen clambered up the hill and set up sniper positions overlooking the wooded area beyond the field upon which they were setting up their camp. A corpsman came over and cut the arms of his shirt with a bayonet, then slit his pants leg before injecting him with morphine. Steve soon slipped into La La Land as the medic began digging bullets out of his body, and eventually he fell unconscious.

He awakened to a bitter cold as night had fallen along the mountainside. He saw a number of small fires covered by ponchos suspended by tree branches to diminish visibility from a distance. His arms and leg were numbed by a stabbing pain and he was very hungry. The soldiers nearby saw him moving around and quickly notified Captain Evilenko.

"It is good to see you have regained consciousness," Evilenko smiled. "We have been discussing your situation and have figured out a way that you will be able to help us."

"How can I possibly help?" Steve wondered as he thanked one of the soldiers for a cup of warm coffee and a bowl of stew.

"We believe that the rebels have yet another lookout on the other side of the cavern leading to the valley where we believe they have set up their underground storage depots," Evilenko explained. "We were fairly certain that you and your friends came out here to investigate rumors of the guerillas bringing captives out here to kill for their organs and body parts. This is also why we have been sent here.

They will be on guard for a military unit, but they will be far less suspicious of a lone man. We will escort you to a designated area where we expect them to be patrolling, and once they move against you we will destroy them."

Steve resignedly took a pistol they gave him and headed back down towards the cavern where they had dragged the bodies of the KLA soldiers just hours ago. It was nearing midnight, and the only light came from the full moon shining brightly overhead as it reflected off the limestone along the ravine. As he entered the cavern he could see that the walls were also covered with limestone, and the mold made it appear incandescent as he saw the bodies of the dead stacked along either side. Almost as an afterthought, he popped the cylinder of the revolver he had been given and saw that it was loaded with silver-jacketed bullets.

He limped over a quarter-mile on his bad leg and felt like giving up. He had seen two of his closest friends murdered just hours ago and was shot himself. The coffee and the bowl of stew had not done much for him, and he was still weak from the loss of blood. His wounds were burning again and each of the injured limbs felt as if they had been stomped on. He shuffled along the limestone trail, not knowing or caring whether he came across the KLA or got caught in a crossfire between the opposing units.

At once he heard a muffled roar, almost like that of a lion in a circus. He stopped in his tracks, peering ahead into the foggy darkness of the tree-shaded lane ahead. He knew he had enough bullets to kill a wild animal, but it would be one less he had with which to defend himself against the KLA, as if a revolver would be enough to defend against automatic rifles. He crept ahead softly, hoping the Serbs were watching closely enough to intervene if he got waylaid by a wild beast.

Suddenly he saw what seemed to be a giant wolf emerging from the shadows ahead. It was hard to tell, but its head appeared as high as Steve's shoulders from the ground. It was of enormous size, possibly about three hundred pounds of muscle and bone. Its eyes were as burning embers and its fangs as ivory daggers as it stared straight at Steve. He broke out into a three-point stance, frozen in place with the revolver at the ready, pointed straight at the monstrous beast. He would empty the pistol at the target as it got within leaping distance, and whatever was left of him would be what the KLA might make do with.

The giant wolf walked over slowly, deliberately, then broke into a rush at once, charging and leaping at Steve as he began pumping the trigger before the great impact swept him into oblivion.

"Still with us, son?"

Steve opened his eyes and beheld a soldier sitting alongside him. He was in a bed, presumably in a hospital, and was somewhat surprised that tubes were not running from every hole in his body. He was even more surprised that all his pains were gone, which made him think he had been here for a very long time. He saw the generic UN helmet on the man's head, recognized the American accent and what Steve considered the shoulder patch of the NWO[1].

"Where am I? How long have I been here?"

"You're in the Main Hospital of Pristina," he replied. "I'm Captain Jude Ryun, United States Army detachment with the UN Peacekeeping Forces. We got a tip from the Serbian Army that a KLA unit was operating along the Prokletije range near Gusinje. We moved in and found you in the middle of a killing field with two squads of KLA men.

You were the only survivor, covered with blood, without a scratch on you. We're still trying to figure out what happened."

"The last thing I remember, I was walking through the valley as a point man for a Serbian Army patrol," Steve sat up in the ramshackle room. The paint was cracked and peeling on both the walls and the furniture. "They had rescued me from a KLA unit and asked me to join them in hunting down the main force. I came across a wolf in the woods and it attacked me. I got off a couple of rounds with the gun I was given, and that's all I remember."

"We found the wolf," Ryun smiled tersely. "He had a chestful of silver bullet slugs in him. I guess that was all about those superstitions up in those mountains. Doesn't look like those KLA guerrillas were as lucky. I suspect National Geographic'll be all over this one. It looked like a pack of wolves got hold of that rebel unit and tore them to pieces. Damnedest thing, though, the only carcass we found was the one you shot. I can't say anyone's upset about the way it went down, but it's the damnedest thing."

"Did you find the---bodies of my friends?"

"Yeah, the Serbs turned them in along with the jeep. We got your camera equipment downstairs, you can pick it up when you leave. Your friends' bodies and personals belongings will be shipped back to their families. I'm sorry about all that."

"So am I," Steve said quietly.

He left the hospital in a state of confusion, astounded that his gunshot wounds had disappeared entirely. The medical staff reported that he was in perfect condition outside of having suffered from exposure and exhaustion. He made arrangements to fly back to New York, and it was that same night when the nightmares began.

He dreamt of that night in the valley, walking along the moonlit path, and being attacked by the giant wolf. Only after he unloaded his weapon into the beast, it sank its teeth into his neck and somehow transferred its spirit into him. He heard the screams and cries of the untold numbers of victims of the beast reverberating through the woods, howling as banshees as they rushed through the wolf's jaws and into Steve's very soul. Steve pushed free and began crawling, only to find himself transforming into the shape of the beast itself. He could not resist the urge to rip his clothes from his body with his teeth, and suddenly he began howling uncontrollably, celebrating the freedom of his spirit as much as an insatiable need for conquest. He needed to go out into the night and establish dominion over the dark places, to claim his place as the lord and master of the wilderness.

They were astounding dreams, the kind that one has to awaken from to believe they had not actually happened. Yet when he woke up, it was all too unsettling, almost as if waking from an alcohol blackout with the terrible realization that things happened that one could not remember. After a while he realized they were happening during the full moon cycle, and he was blacking out just after the moon reached its apex in the night sky. He began staying home and locking himself in his room in those times, but the nightmares kept recurring and he dared not reach out to anyone for help.

It was over a decade later when he met Mirjana Dragana. It was at that time when he realized he could harness the power.

It was then that he realized he could return evil for evil.

CHAPTER THREE

"It was absolutely horrible, Steve!" Jana wept as they sat in the small but cozy living room of her loft apartment on Prince Street, right down the hall from his. "I'll never forget the sight of it. The screams and cries will be with me for as long as I live!"

"What did you see?" he wondered. She had been wiped out on tranquilizers since her return from the hospital, and it was the next evening before she phoned and asked him to come over. He saw she had been crying, and he guessed that she had probably loaded up on sedatives to help calm her nerves from the incident as well as the coke withdrawal.

"It was a dog, but much larger," she wiped her reddened eyes with a kerchief. "It was even larger than a wolf. I know how things get mixed up and people's minds play tricks on them in times of stress. I have plenty of experience with that from the war in Serbia. Yet there are things that I know I saw, things that I cannot deny."

"Like what?" he asked gently.

"The---the beast, it stood on its hind legs like a man," she focused hard, trying to remember all the details. "It broke down the door the way a man would, but charged into the room like an animal, on all fours. It headed straight for Kane, and even though his friends had pulled their pistols out and were shooting at it, the bullets seemed to have no effect. They were hitting the animal, but they could not stop it. The bullets were not passing through, they were penetrating but with no effect."

"Did all the men have guns? Did they all shoot the wolf?"

"Yes, they did, the carpet was covered with shell casings," she said with a soft Serbian accent. "There must have been over sixty shots fired in minutes. Yet the animal jumped on Kane and ripped his throat out with one bite. It was like a steel trap, it didn't seem real, none of it. It turned and jumped at the next man, then the next. It happened so fast that no one had time to react. You've seen how fast animals react in the wild; it was just like what happened in that room. The beast just raced from one person to the next as if it was tearing meat from hooks in a butcher's shop. There was no way to fight it, it was strong as a bear."

"Where did it go?" Steve asked. "Did it know you were in the room?"

"It ran right back out the door. There was no way I could have possibly looked to see where it went, I was frozen with terror. I remember it looked straight at me, and I can assure you it was like looking into the eyes of the Devil. It was like the eyes of a serpent, only they were glowing red as if on fire. It also had fangs like a serpent, only they were like blades, and dripping with blood from those men it killed. Its jaws, its chest, its paws and legs were covered in blood. It looked into my eyes almost like it knew me. It was the longest and most terrifying moment of my life. It just stared as if it was trying to communicate with me, then all of a sudden it turned and rushed through the door, and it was gone."

"What questions did the police ask? Did they give you any idea as to what they were looking for? All the newspapers said that there were signs of an attack dog having been let loose in the room."

"That is almost a joke, a terrible joke," she shook her head. "One dog could not have done such a thing. Besides, the dogs would have had to have been bulletproof. That was the worst part of all. They acted as if I was lying, or I had been hysterical throughout the whole time. There was one fellow, a detective, he was a Serbian and he tried to be condescending. You know, trying to talk to me in Serbian, but he'd been away too long and he made himself look the fool. We ended up speaking in English, and he asked me all about the beast. He taped the conversation on his little recorder and he took notes on his pad, then he left. I was taken from the building straight to the hospital, and they did not let me out until this morning."

"Do you remember his name?"

"It was Darko something. I'm sure I have his card around here somewhere."

"Darko," Steve exhaled softly.

"Do you know this fellow?" she asked.

"I've come across him from time to time," Steve allowed. "Do you remember how I told you that I was free-lancing near Kosovo during the war? Well, I had quite a bit of contact with the KLA while I was there. I don't know how much you've heard about the atrocities the Muslims were committing along the Accursed Mountains near West Kosovo."

"I lived there during the war, Steve," she smiled wryly. "I'm afraid I've seen far more than I have heard."

"It was rumored that the KLA was bringing captives to hidden laboratories in the mountains where they were being killed for their body parts," Steve said hesitantly. "The KLA was harvesting their organs for transplants, selling them to the Chinese. I had heard about it and decided to investigate on my own. I gathered evidence but eventually attracted the attention of KLA units in the area. They hunted me down and were going to kill me, but I was rescued by Serbian Army units under Colonel Evilenko."

"Evilenko," she gasped, her lovely eyes wide with trepidation.

"You've heard of him?"

"He was known as the Beast of the Black Mountains, the *Crna Gora*," she winced at the memory. "It is very hard to explain this to outsiders, people who are not from Serbia. You must remember that the people of this region lived side by side for hundreds of years, but there are always those who will dredge up ancient rivalries whenever an old wound is reopened. There were times at the turn of the century when the Muslims and the Albanians persecuted the Orthodox Christians in the area. Some of the stories were terrible, but no one would hold the descendants of the guilty parties responsible after so many years passed. No one but the fanatics who people like Evilenko rallied behind them. They claimed they were avenging the murder of our people, but it became clear their only purpose was to steal, kill and destroy."

"I saw what Evilenko and his men did," Steve said ruefully. "They never let me take any photos of what they did. They kept my equipment with them from the time they picked me up to the time I left. Unfortunately when they released me, my camera was destroyed and I had no evidence against the underground organ traders when I returned to the States. Somehow that detective Darko got a lead on me, and he's been on my case ever since."

"You don't think---he came after me because of you?"

"No, I think he got onto you because you're Serbian," Steve replied. "You know how the police try and entrap people by using others of their own kind to get information. They're probably seeing this as a drug killing and looking to see if you knew anything about it."

"Why? Why would they think---?" she grew frightened.

"They're cops, they get paid to look at people," he assured her. "There was a dog killing a few months ago, it was all over the news, remember? They never came up with anything else, so they're scrambling for leads again. I'm sure they checked your story and saw you were there on business. Why else would a beautiful actress like you be in the same building with a slimeball like Kane North?"

"Well, I, uh---" she managed, having been caught completely off-guard. "As it turns out, Mr. North happened to be one of the major investors in the movie project I was involved in. When the production was called off, I made a number of inquiries and eventually I was put in touch with Mr. North. Of course, I was aware of his reputation, but I also know that many former drug dealers were able to invest their money in legitimate enterprises and have turned their lives and fortunes around. They say it is much like the bootleggers of the past century here in America. I'm just trying to find my own way, I'm in no position to judge others."

"I don't know if I'd lump Kane North in alongside the Kennedys," Steve managed a smile. "I'd just be worried about someone like you associating with people like that. He doesn't seem to hold women in the highest esteem. He produced his own records, among other things, and lots of his lyrics were almost misogynistic in nature. I think I would've been very concerned if you had become part of his circle."

"Thank you, Steve," she lowered her eyes before gazing into his earnestly. "I know you are my friend and that you care about me. You know, I think about you a lot and thank God that I have someone like you living next door to me that I can confide in."

"Anytime you ever need anything, you know all you have to do is ask," he replied quietly. He knew he was falling in love with her but did not dare pursue a relationship with her. He felt as if she was too emotionally vulnerable, and had too much on her plate with her drug dependence to go into a relationship right now. Plus he was still living with the *curse*, and that was nothing he could ever dare visit upon someone he loved.

He rose from the armchair in which he sat across from her loveseat and came around the glass-topped coffee table as she stood to escort him to the door. He held her hands as she lowered her head shyly. He knew she was expecting him to try and kiss her, but he released her hands and walked over to the door.

"You get some sleep," he smiled at her. "You've had way too much on your plate the last couple of days."

"Thanks, Steve," she smiled back. "Good night."

She stared wistfully at the door long after he was gone.

It was very much like being an alcoholic, or alcohol intolerant. At first it was total blackout, then after the end of the first year he remembered bits and pieces of what had happened. By the end of the fifth year it was like being roaring drunk, having almost no control of one's faculties and slipping in and out of awareness. Over the last couple of years it was like driving drunk, somehow being able to manage control though quite often having sudden lapses. He began taking the Amtrak to the Catskills in New York or the Poconos in Pennsylvania during the full moon cycle, and renting a cabin in remote areas for the duration.

He would let the dog out before midnight, leaving a key and spare clothing hidden outside the cabin and locking the door before he went out into the woods. He would go deeper and deeper, as far as he could get, to the most secluded area where no one in their right mind would venture in the dark. In the past couple of years he could remember the change, and would remove his clothes so that he might be able to find them the next day, and recollect the process.

The metamorphosis itself was the hardest part, as if going into insulin shock. He would fall writhing into convulsions, experiencing the most retching sickness. Just before he could no longer endure it, it was gone. He would rise from his own ashes as a supreme being, incredibly powerful, agile and quick, though his brain was as a drunk that could barely recall lifting his glass from the table. He would run as a boy realizing his adolescence, one day able to run and jump with muscles he did not know he had. He would run and climb to where no other being dared venture, and when he arrived along the craggiest bluff at the highest peak, he would howl at the moon in triumphant exultation.

He found he could hunt in the night, and often crept down to the campgrounds like an Indian counting coup. It was the game he played and never lost, sneaking down and touching a sleeping bag, putting his head into a tent, and even stealing food without anyone knowing he was there. Those who brought dogs were the easiest to avoid, as his scent would drive them berserk when he came within a hundred yards. When there were no dogs, his own sense of smell was as a radar that could detect a human at that same hundred yards' radius.

His hearing was just as keen, and it took him a long time to overcome the overwhelming sense of paranoia that came with knowing one was completely surrounded by living things. Discernment came in time, and he could distinguish dangerous creatures from rodents and wild game. He soon learned that bears had a live and let live attitude towards him, mountain lions avoided him, and other wolves saw him as a mortal threat. It greatly encouraged him, but even in his surreal state of inebriation, he knew that his life could be ended by one man with a gun. In this, he was no different than any other creature in the forest.

The most frightening aspect was the craving for blood, and this was more real than any he had ever known. It was like a maddening thirst in the throes of dehydration, a searing hunger after days of fasting, a tormenting itch that one would tear their skin to relieve. It often caused him to black out, and when he awoke to find himself devouring a small creature, it was as a ravenous man reconciling himself to eating cooked food that had fallen on the ground. He was terrified to think what could happen if he was in a populated area, much like a drunk driver trapped amidst a four-lane highway at night during rush hour.

Over the past few years his moments of clarity had helped him turn some of his absurd episodes into memorable experiences. He went from voyeurism in watching pretty women making love from the shadows, to stopping date rapes and even gang rapes. He helped searchers find lost persons, and even rescued people by helping them find their way or items that facilitated their escape. It was then that he realized he could use the phenomenon for good, and he only needed to be creative in channeling its resource.

He learned that the beast was invincible when he came across gangbangers assaulting a young couple just a few years ago, when he started to be able to remember things as if in short video clips. They were carrying automatic weapons, and they opened up fire on him as he emerged from the bushes. He had watched them pull the couple out of their parked car, beating up the young man before stripping the girl and spreading her naked onto the grass. He began snarling and growling from the shadows, stopping the attack before he revealed himself. They opened up fire and he rolled away in fear, feeling the slugs tear into his face and chest. He ran away for a distance until he realized he had not been injured. He went back and saw that the gangbangers had fled, leaving the couple to regroup, thanking God that the creature had come and saved their lives.

One day he realized that the beast could very well be a time bomb that could be set to detonate in a place of evil at the appointed time. He knew that if he found a place of refuge in the heart of darkness when the full moon rose, the beast would emerge and they would not be able to withstand it. He thought long and hard about it, and did much research before coming to a decision. He knew that if the beast was captured or killed, his secret would come to light at dawn when the possession waned from him. He no longer cared at that point whether he lived or died, so he would accept whatever came upon him.

He had researched demonic possession as soon as he came back to America from Kosovo. He spoke to Catholic priests, then evangelical Christians, even *brujos* from the black magic Santeria cults among the Caribbean people of NYC. They all told him that the demon could be exorcised if only he believed. Steve, an agnostic, knew he was beyond hope as he did not believe. He knew that all he could do was live with the curse and make the best of it as he could. Bringing it to the predators and destroyers seemed the logical thing.

He learned of the 137th Street Gang in East Harlem, among the most ruthless killers in the nation. They controlled the crack trade in the area and held the community in a grip of terror despite concerted efforts by the NYPD to bring them down. Drive-by shootings were costing the lives of innocent victims, and the killing of a six-year-old schoolgirl prompted Steve to action.

He dressed as a vagrant, picking up some rags at the Salvation Army the day before the full moon cycle began. He picked out a beanie, a hoodie, faded jeans and combat boots, knowing the beast would tear them off in due time. He knew the beast could find a place of refuge, and hopefully it would be somewhere he could literally cover his ass at daybreak. He waited until sunset, taking a train to East Harlem and looking around for a place to hide near the crack houses. There was a urine-soaked, garbage-strewn alley where he found trash cans to sit behind. He closed his eyes and went into a dozing state of meditation until he finally blacked out.

He found himself beneath the Manhattan Bridge the next morning near a vagrant camp that had been deserted for the day. He was able to grab a pair of socks, a shirt and pants from one of the dozens of bindles left by the homeless who camped there. He rushed back to Soho on aching feet, realizing for the first time just what it was like for a man on the streets of New York without a penny to his name.

The media proclaimed what he had done in whirlwind coverage of the event. It was rumored that a rival drug gang attacked the 137th Streeters overnight, ripping them up in a vicious attack using what appeared to be axes, knives and machetes. The episode was so quick that witnesses outside the building said the entire struggle lasted no more than a couple of minutes. The Mayor's Office and the NYPD condemned the ferocity of the attack and assured the public that gang violence in East Harlem was soon coming to an end.

It was shortly after that Mirjana Dragona moved into the loft, and he immediately fell in love though he knew this was Beauty and the Beast. He could never let anyone into his life knowing that the beast would forever stand between them. Yet he got as close to Jana as he dared, and as he stood by helplessly and watched her life descend into chaos, he swore that he would never abide by anyone abusing her or hurting her. When her crack connection became too familiar with her and began appearing on her doorstep to take liberties, the night came that he and his gang had to answer. It was on that night that Darko Lucic made the connection and began looking at Steve Lurgan.

Now he was faced with disappearing from the sight of Detective Lucic, and in doing so, abandoning the friend he swore to never forsake. He knew that would never happen, and only hoped for Lucic's sake that he, like so many others before him, would not place himself in a position to stare into the eyes of the monster from the Abyss.

CHAPTER FOUR

Captain Bojan Evilenko had been the leader of Company Z, a top-secret paratrooper unit created by direct order of President Radovan Karadzic. They were an anti-insurgent unit assigned to exterminate all terrorist groups operating in the Sar Mountains near Kosovo. They experienced some of the most brutal fighting in the war as the militants had been taking hostages and holding them for ransom. When rescuers drew nigh, they would use the hostages as human shields in making their escape deeper into the mountains. The Serbians' greatest concern was over the rumors that the Albanians were dissecting hostages in hidden laboratories, harvesting their organs and body parts for sale to the Chinese.

Evilenko had heard the rumors of the werewolf of the Accursed Mountains, and had seen evidence of its depredations as it left corpses behind like no other. Lost troops had been killed by wild animals before, but ones who encountered the werewolf were literally torn to shreds. The bite marks appeared as gashes caused by bear traps, which he knew would have been impossible to use in such a fashion.

He played a wild hunch in sending the American journalist out with a gun loaded with silver bullets on that full moon night long ago. He and his friends were nothing out of the ordinary. They were foolish young people out to tamper with the legends and superstitions of the country, and more often than not they came across wild beasts whose savagery perpetuated the wives' tales. Only the werewolf was something even the military could not disprove, and using the American in yet another experiment finally paid off.

When he came across the demonic beast and became possessed by its spirit, he charged blindly into the wilderness and headed straight into the enemy stronghold which was not far from Gusinje. He ripped them to pieces and headed straight into the woods, giving Evilenko the opportunity to call the UN Peacekeeping Forces and report the incident. The New World Order troops cleaned up what was left of the KLA platoon, then rescued Lurgan in the woods the next morning.

Evilenko followed up on the newly-acquired information and not only located the rebel base, but the hidden laboratory in a mountain cave. He acquired all their medical and computer equipment as well as vital organs and body parts carefully preserved and prepared for shipment. He contacted the Chinese and informed them that he was now in control, and that business could continue as usual as long as payments were all made to Evilenko via a Swiss bank account. The Chinese had no choice, and made arrangements to accommodate their new business partner.

Evilenko and his men captured the mad scientists who were performing the vivisections, and gave them an ultimatum to work for the Serbians under pain of gruesome death. They all readily agreed, as they had been coerced to work for the Albanians far beyond the terms of the initial agreement. The Captain then ordered his men to continue operating in the same manner as had the Albanians. They would bring their captives back here and turn them over to the scientists for harvesting before execution. It was but a short time before the murder machine was operating at peak capacity once again.

Once the war ended, Evilenko was forced to initiate evacuation plans as both President Karadzic and General Mladic had been arrested by the NWO and charged with crimes against humanity. He made an agreement with the Chinese that he and his men, along with the scientists, would be extracted from the country and provided with false documents allowing their emigration to the USA. The Chinese government, colluding with the criminal Tong organization, facilitated the move through the efforts of the Ministry of State Security[1]. The entire operation was relocated from the Sar Mountains to the Catskills in upstate New York under the guise of a Chinese computer programming and development company.

The immediate problem facing Evilenko and his men was the inadequate supply of donors after leaving the war zone. Their solution was to take advantage of the homeless situation in New York City, offering to relocate them for research programs in exchange for room and board. Some of the victims of the scam were teenagers runaways, and when it was suspected they had been murdered, NYPD Homicide and Darko Lucic stepped into the picture.

The Tong had ethnic Chinese working in the Department, and they were able to access restricted case files with the aid of some of the most proficient hackers on the planet in the MSS. They broke into the Homicide files and discovered that Lucic was assigned to the missing persons case. He had found that more than a few of the missing teens had been buried in the Catskill Mountains, and that some of their vital organs had been surgically removed. The evidence was added to a compilation in a growing case file on the Chinese Tong, which was under investigation by INTERPOL for organ trafficking. Lucic, aware that the KLA had been a major resource for the Tong in Kosovo, began focusing his search in that direction.

When the Serbian mercenaries learned that Lucic was looking at Lurgan, they immediately informed Evilenko. The Captain was gifted with a photographic memory, remembering Lurgan and the circumstances surrounding their encounter over ten years ago. "He is here," Evilenko stared into the starry sky. "Fate has proclaimed that we would be reunited after surviving the brutal struggle and the living hell of Kosovo. We will bring him here and bring him into the Sacred Circle. He will become a White Knight of the Serbian Empire, bringing honor and glory to our race and our nation unto the end of time."

Upon leaving Serbia, Evilenko and his men joined an underground movement sworn to protect and defend its people against its enemies, particularly the Muslims who continued to foment revolution throughout the country. The Captain retained his rank in the militant group, and pledged to send ten percent of the operation's income to the Knights in exchange for asylum should they be forced to flee America. Evilenko felt he had all his bases covered, and would strive to bring Lurgan into the fold as his field specialist. After what Evilenko witnessed in the Accursed Mountains, he knew there was nothing the NYPD had that could prevail against him.

Darko Lucic knew that he was not going to get anything out of Steve Lurgan unless he had hard evidence to hold against his throat. Even though Lurgan was a journalist, he had been in combat situations for the better part of a decade and was not going to bend under pressure. He knew that Jana Dragana was his weak link, but he did not want to go that route just yet. He detested the kinds of cops that operated in that fashion. He always felt that it was the lazy cop's way out. If a good detective had a suspect cornered so that such a weak link was found, it just took extra pressure and hard work to make more cracks appear.

Homicide was working a sting operation on a Russian Mob crew that was suspected of organ trafficking with the Chinese Tong in Lower Manhattan. The Russians were allegedly abducting stowaways at the New York harbor and sending them to underground laboratories for organ harvesting. Lucic had a hunch that the Serbians would probably be working with the Russians as best they could. Neither side could afford to end up with people waiting in line outside their labs for processing. They were only a few steps away from having the Feds involved in a serial murder investigation. Lucic and his superiors had no doubt that the Chinese would do whatever it took to burn the bridge behind it.

Lucic and his partner, Benny Tracker, had been looking at a low-level Serbian hood who worked the docks near Chinatown as a bookie and loan shark. Ilija Ljubica had served in the Army under Ratko Mladic and fled to avoid the UN investigation of suspected war criminals. He migrated to the USA and immediately made contact with fellow veterans who had found work with the Russian Mob. He had moved up the ranks by way of his physical prowess and ruthlessness in dealing with delinquent accounts. The Russians had not offered him full membership as yet but were comfortable with him moving large chunks of cash around for them.

Tracker was a Puerto Rican of Apache descent who had

served as a Marine in Iraq and had no problem getting around on the streets of New York. He pulled the Ford Contour along the curb next to where Ljubica was walking down the street, and Ilija was about to cut and run before Lucic flashed his badge from the passenger window.

"Get in, let's take a little ride and have a chat," Lucic called over in Serbian.

"Bullshit," Ljubica tensed for flight.

"Look, we can do this here or at the station, either way," Lucic snapped in street English. Ljubica shrugged and got in the back seat of the car.

"You see this kid around?" Tracker handed an 8"x11" glossy back to Ljubica.

"Nope. Never," he handed it right back.

"Look, don't hand me no shit," Lucic grabbed it and tossed it back in Ljubica's lap. "Maybe you haven't seen him but I know you're looking for him. He can identify Evilenko, and probably his top guys from Kosovo. He was on the Prokletije range near Gusinje with the Captain and his men in 1999 at the end of the war. I've got him on the spot for those dog killings in East Harlem, and he's talking like a parrot on crack. He's getting ready to connect the dots between your people and the Chinese Tong and that body shop they're running up in the Catskills."

"Whoa, wait a second," Ljubica chortled in disbelief. "You're trying to tag me a long way from home. I take bets and lend money once in a while, but you don't have anything connecting me to a body shop or whatever you call it."

"Let's see what else I got," Lucic turned around and rested his chin on his hands over the backrest. "I got your main man Mikhail Fetisov getting set up on RICO charges for money laundering and tax evasion with that bogus export corporation he set up in Montreal. I got five of his top guys going down with him, and when I start trading for time off, I'll bet you they'll gladly give you up to get a couple of years knocked off their sentence. That puts your ass on a boat back home, where they send you to the Hague on a war crimes charge."

"I really don't think it'll be that easy," Ljubica shook his head smilingly.

"Maybe not, but right now you're the best lead I got and I'm the only friend you got. Lurgan's holding a leash for some dangerous people, and I need to know how I can get him off the street. You need to tell me why Evilenko's looking for Lurgan."

"They are not looking for the man who controls the beast. They are looking for the beast himself."

"So they believe that the beast is a man? How stupid do you think I am?"

"It does not matter what you believe. Anyone who lived near the Accursed Mountains near the Labyrinths of Hell knew of the beast that came from the abyss. It took men's souls for hundreds of years until one day a man came and destroyed the beast. He became possessed by the demon and took the spirit of the beast away to a foreign land. Evilenko has found the beast and now wishes to control its power."

"What's this guy talking about?" Tracker turned to Lucic. "What's he smoking?"

"Okay, this is for real," Lucic spoke in Serbian again. "You're trying to tell me that Evilenko really thinks Lurgan is a werewolf."

"You know, you're living in an age where air forces around the world are sighting UFO's, where serial killers are drinking the blood of their victims, and people are rebuilding others with body parts of the dead," Ljubica was derisive. "All of the superstitions of the past are being proven as fact in this century. What makes it so hard to think that a man with a personality disorder cannot manifest the qualities of a wild animal? It takes no great stretch of the imagination to think such a man can be put to use within specialized organizations."

"First you're talking beasts and abysses, now you're on about personality disorders. I need to know what Evilenko is saying."

"I have never met Evilenko, I only know what his people want others to know. He knows Lurgan is living somewhere here in Manhattan and wishes to speak with him. He believes in the power of the beast. Whether he thinks there is a living monster I do not know."

"Well, the Captain certainly has fed you guys some line of shit," Lucic reverted to English for Tracker's benefit. "Look, here's my card. You call me if you find out anything about Evilenko contacting Lurgan, and vice versa. You do me that favor and I'll let you know when they're set to let the hammer down on Fetisov."

"Are you gonna be able to get me off the hook?" he asked as he got out of the car.

"No, but we'll let you know when it's time to leave town," Lucic assured him before they drove off.

"So what was all that about? Tracker wondered as they cruised back towards Police Plaza near City Hall.

"Bunch of Old Country bullshit," Lucic exhaled tautly. "They got one hand on their keyboard and the other hand on their crucifix. I told you about all that superstitious crap Lurgan got caught up with near Kosovo. To this day, people near Gusinje talk about the American who went into the mountains and killed the werewolf. I'm betting that

Evilenko's trying to use those superstitions to his advantage over here."

"Who'd buy into that shit?" Benny smirked.

"Practically every immigrant sneaking into this country, plus more than a few who've been here for a while. Every country's got their old wives' tales of demon possession. Plus, you've got a *brujo*, or a *miali*[2], or even a Catholic priest on every block ready to back it up. Evilenko's gonna use Lurgan to enforce his code of silence, unless we get to Lurgan first and make him see things our way."

"Get to Lurgan? You don't have his address?"

"He went into the wind sometime last week," Lucic stared out the window at the Manhattan skyline as they hit the highway. "No one knows where he is, not even the next-door neighbor he's got the hots for. His lease is paid up for the year, so he comes back when he feels like it. I can't stake him out on a hunch. All I can hope is that if I can't find him, Evilenko can't either."

Steve Lurgan heard that there were a couple of Serbians asking for him, and he immediately called Jana and told her he would be out of town for a couple of weeks to look into a job offer on the West Coast. Steve told her that he had made quite a bit of money in Serbia during the war and was still living off royalties he was being paid for exclusive photos he took. His savings and investments had worn thin over time, and he would eventually have to get back to work in order to renew his lease. He didn't know if Jana would betray the confidence and air his dirty laundry before strangers, but it certainly would cover his tracks if she did.

He rented a room at a Bowery flophouse, one of the few still in existence, and brought the kind of rucksack he took along during his road trips across Serbia. He decided to lay low and run recon on his own loft for a few days to find out who was looking for him and for what reason. He owed no man from his days in Kosovo and expected no one to come looking for him. The only thing he could imagine was bounty hunters looking for any one of the men now listed as war criminals. He had nothing to tell them, but wanted to be ready for someone who would come insisting that he did.

The full moon was a couple of weeks away, and it was as serious a deadline as for a man awaiting his execution date. There was no way around this, no way of intoxicating, sedating, binding or locking oneself up. He would never forget chaining himself with a titanium-link product, only to find it broken when he returned the following day to the place where he had locked himself up. He needed to take the beast as far away from civilization as possible lest it do what it did when confronted by the drug dealers just weeks ago. It was something he was a long, long way from being able to control.

He considered the notion that the damned thing seemed to be indestructible. If it wasn't for the monster attached, it would be a true blessing for someone with a handicap or an incurable disease. He realized that lots of his maladies and genetic defects had disappeared over time, and many of his physical qualities had improved over the past decade. He had a couple of pinhole cavities that had disappeared, scars from his childhood that had vanished, and other little things like never getting headaches, colds or flu. If there was some way to tap into this thing, it could possibly cure cancer. He would have turned himself in a long time ago, but chances are they would lock him away for the rest of his days, like some little green man from a flying saucer landing in New Mexico.

One thing that truly frightened him was the thought that if someone found out about the curse, they would be able to use the knowledge of the full moon cycle to their advantage. If they wanted to get to Jana for whatever reason and knew that he went on hiatus during the cycle, there would not be a damn thing he could do about it. He had timed his attack on the drug dealers so that he returned from upstate on the last day of the cycle. Afterwards he spent sleepless nights wondering what might have happened if he had miscalculated at any point.

He fell into a melancholy mood as he reflected on the fact that he was, indeed, like a stray dog having been cast out from his home into the streets. He could only sneak back onto Prince Street from a distance and watch his neighbors go in and out of his loft building. He watched in trepidation as strangers passed by, worried that one of them would be of those who were looking for him. He hoped that they would not turn Jana against him with offers of money or drugs. It would be a betrayal he would not be able to live with.

His entire life had been cast into turmoil after leaving Serbia. He realized this more than ever, as if the chaos of war was like a stain on his soul that would never go away. It was not just the beast, as if that were not more than enough, but all of the implications such as his loneliness and his inability to share his burden or discuss his plight with anyone. He had suffered just as much as any soldier who had fought in the war, and was paying a higher price than anyone could ever imagine.

He only hoped that death was not the only solution in taking the pain away.

CHAPTER FIVE

If Jana Dragana knew of Steve Lurgan's inner turmoil, she would have questioned whether the demon tormenting him was that much worse than the one that hounded her. She would have argued that at least his demon only plagued him during the full moon cycle. It did not come at him every single day.

She was struggling mightily to overcome her crack addiction. She had been a willful girl from her youth, confident in her natural beauty and the spirit to overcome obstacles in her life. Growing up in Bosnia exposed her to racial and economic tension, though her looks helped her sidestep most of the snares that her friends often fell victim to. She knew that she had to leave Serbia if she was ever to build a future for herself, and eventually migrated to the Czech Republic where she learned a new language as well as improved upon her English. From there she got into modeling and made her way to England. It took a couple of years before she saved up enough to cross the Atlantic, and New York City became the challenge of her life.

At first she was on a roll as she signed up with a

modeling agency and picked up enough high-paying assignments to pay for a one-year lease on a Prince Street loft in Soho. Only her ego got in the way as the smooth-talkers began steering her into the fast lane. They assured her that her beauty would certainly take her to Hollywood, and invited her to exclusive parties that made her feel that she was reaching that next level. Only the drugs were planned to break her will, and her lack of discernment led her to involvement with street dealers who began leading her down a blind alley of dependency.

The connection provided by her agent at Unchained Productions was a Rocco Friddi, who was a mid-level crack dealer who was notorious for taking advantage of female addicts short of funds to support their habit. It was right around the time she made friends with her next-door neighbor, Steve Lurgan. Steve was a handsome man who claimed to be a photojournalist living off his earnings from covering the Serbian War. He was very secretive yet friendly, and did not pry beyond whatever information she gave him. Rocco and Steve did not seem to like each other, but they remained respectful of one another until the day came when Rocco disappeared from her life.

She phoned her agent and asked if he had heard from Rocco, and the response was that he had been killed but no one knew what had happened. She dared not ask for another reference, and the vibes she was getting indicated that such a request might not have been welcome at that particular time. She began drinking heavily to quench her cravings, and her agent sensed what was happening when he did not hear from her. He reached out to Kane North, turning him on to her webpage and telling him what a hottie she was. He killed two birds with one stone in connecting Jana with North, but now Kane was dead and Jana was going through her crack withdrawal again. Her agent was wondering whether he should give her up as a dead-end prospect.

Jana was feeling hopeless now that her dealer was dead, her producer was also gone, and her friend Steve had left town. The thought of getting a regular job was ludicrous, but she was wondering if this was her only option. She had only a few hundred dollars of savings left, and it would barely cover her expenses for the month. She was surfing the Internet non-stop for days on end, but all the e-mail queries were rejected as quickly as she sent them.

She heard a knock on the door on this particular afternoon, and eventually opened at the sound of a Serbian accent outside. Ilija Ljubica introduced himself as a representative of Herzegovina Programming Solutions, a high-tech computer software developer out of the Catskills in upstate New York. He informed her that they had gotten her information from a modeling agency she had contacted. HPS was looking for someone to fill an executive secretary position. The ideal candidate would be proficient at clerical work as well as dealing directly with clients as a company representative. Her modeling skills would be a strong attribute, and they were certain that her clerical skills would be enhanced by training and experience.

"This is just wonderful news," she gushed as she brought Ljubica a cup of coffee. She was greatly impressed by the man's military demeanor, his rugged good looks and his way of expressing himself. "I was getting so worried about finding something. Of course, my first love is modeling, and I'm sure you are aware that my agency is trying to find a position that will further my career."

"My employer anticipated that, and authorized me to offer one hundred thousand dollars as a yearly salary,"

Ljubica replied. "Should you accept the offer, your first check will be electronically deposited in your bank account. We will pay you on a monthly basis by the first of the month. You will also be provided with room and board at the Company's expense."

"Will I be working weekends?" she wondered. "I wouldn't want to leave the Manhattan area entirely, what with this apartment and all."

"I believe that the owner of the Company wants to meet with you to finalize the agreement and review the minute details. He is staying at the Waldorf, I can give you his number so you can set up an interview."

After Ljubica left, Jana called the number on the business card forthwith. She reached one of the secretaries who took her information and confirmed her appointment for six PM that evening. She was walking on air as she put on one of her prettiest business suits and readied for her appointment. She figured that even after taxes, she should be able to draw over a thousand dollars a week from her account. It would definitely be enough to tide her over until her next modeling or acting job came in. She could not wait until Steve came back. She knew he never answered his cell phone if he carried it at all. She hoped he would be back before she headed upstate. If he had not returned by then, she would slip a letter under his door.

She arrived at the elegant hotel and was informed by the manager that her party was expecting her at the Bull and Bear Steakhouse in the lobby complex. She hurried over to the maitre'd, who escorted her to a rear table in the darkened, wood-paneled restaurant where her benefactor awaited.

"Good evening," he stood and shook her hand, kissing it as was the Old Country custom. "I am Zora Vlasic. I am the

CEO and Executive President of HPS. Please have a seat. Would you care for something to drink?"

Vlasic stood 6'2" and weighed 210 pounds of sinewy muscle. His graying hair was receding, his mustache and goatee neatly trimmed. He wore a $1,000 designer suit that was meticulously tailored to fit his athletic build. His blue eyes simmered with energy as he gazed intently at Jana across the table in their corner booth. Jana ordered an iced tea, having learned long ago that one never mixed alcohol with business. People in power tended to look down at subordinates who did so, and she would not make that mistake with this man.

"I am not sure how much Mr. Ljubica told you about the Company," he folded his hands on the table. "We have experienced rapid expansion after the war, enabling us to develop our contacts with other companies from the European Union. Fortunately, we were able to expand our network to include corporations in Russia and China, and they have helped us to significantly improve the quality of our products. We are now very competitive both in Europe and here in the States, and are relying on personal sales to help us gain ground on the leaders in our field."

"It sounds very exciting. I'm looking forward to contributing any way I can."

"We are expecting prospective clients to be making personal visits to our headquarters to see what the Company is all about," Vlasic revealed. "We would have a need for a personable young lady used to interacting with clients and making a favorable impression. I am sure you will do just fine."

Vlasic informed her that he would be e-mailing the application and tax forms to be returned, and would have someone from the corporate headquarters in Catskill contact her tomorrow. They would give her full details as to her travel arrangements and accommodations in order for her to start work Monday. She would also have weekends off unless an event required her attendance, in which case her salary would be adjusted accordingly.

Jana thanked him profusely before leaving, and Vlasic remained behind working on the laptop and a portfolio he had brought with him. He remained alone for a short time before he was joined at length by a new arrival.

"I saw her leave a few minutes ago, Captain," Ilija Ljubica took a seat where Jana had been a short time ago. "I presume everything went according to plan. She seemed very enthusiastic."

"I would have to agree," Bojan Evilenko replied in Serbian. "I am quite sure that when Lurgan comes out of hiding and finds she has left for the Catskills, he will find some way to follow her up there to make sure she is doing well. Once he arrives, we will intercept him and bring him to our headquarters where will make our proposal."

"My only concern would be that damned cop, Lucic," Ljubica scowled. "The nosy bastard rousted me on the street in Chinatown last night. He's hot on the trail of Lurgan, he's trying to tie those dog killings to his tail. If you're trying to bring Lurgan in with the Knights, perhaps it is best that you get him out of the City and away from Lucic. Cops like that are like hot tar. Once they get on you they're almost impossible to remove."

"In this business I have learned that everyone is useful," Evilenko smiled. "Even Albanian dwarves have reusable parts."

The two men shared a knowing laugh.

Steve Lurgan was about five miles away from where Jana had taken leave of Bojan Evilenko. He had walked by the loft on Prince Street and saw that Jana had left on her small lamp in the living room of her second floor apartment, which meant she had probably stepped out. He had no idea that Darko Lucic had made him until the midnight blue Contour pulled up to the curb alongside him.

"Looks like you're lost," Lucic called from the passenger window. "Give you a ride?"

"No, I'm fine," Steve waved him off.

"Get in."

Steve reluctantly clambered into the back seat, and Benny Tracker took off on a leisurely cruise towards the Village.

"How's that girlfriend of yours? Heard from her lately?"

"No, haven't seen her. She's not my girlfriend, I already told you."

"Wishful thinking, huh? Why don't you lighten up? It's a nice night."

"Well, it was just great until you came along," Steve grunted.

"Hey, Benny, pull over. Whyn't you get us all some coffee?"

"Yessir, massa. Can I massage your ass when I get back?"

"G'wan," Lucic snapped as Tracker parked the car and headed for a nearby deli.

"Don't you have any drug dealers or pimps you can screw around with?" Steve was exasperated.

"Nah, I've been busting balls on loan sharks the last few days," Lucic retorted. "Guy named Ilija Ljubica. Sergeant with the First Infantry under General Mladic. Heard of him?"

"Now, do you think I spent my spare time over there memorizing names, ranks and serial numbers?"

"This guy you might be interested in. I think he may be screwing around with that chick you've got your eyes on."

"You know, you're so full of shit, Lucic. If you're not taking me downtown then I'm outta here."

"Okay, try this on. Ljubica's a bottom-feeder with the Russian Mob, but he's still connected to Bojan Evilenko from the Old Country. He was up to see Jana, and we stuck with him and tailed him to the Waldorf a couple of hours later. Turned out that she showed up there about a half hour after Ljubica. Benny went inside and looked around, and she was sitting up in a booth at the Bull and Bear with Evilenko."

"Bastards," Steve's eyes grew misty as he turned away from Darko, staring out the window sightlessly.

"Why don't you just forget about her, Lurgan? You're not a stupid man and you're not naïve. You've been around the world. She's lost, you can't save her from herself. Come out of the ether and step away from this, look at it from the outside for once. People have lost their lives because of her. I don't care whether they deserved it or not, they still died before they had a chance to make good. Nobody---nobody--- has a right to take a man's life until he gets that last chance to make good. If Jana's causing people to die, you got to walk away from her."

"I love her, Darko. I know what she is. I love her. I can't stop loving her."

"So you're gonna let Evilenko use her against you. You're gonna let him manipulate you into letting him get near that beastmaster connection of yours."

"I'm not going to let anything happen to Jana," Steve was determined.

"Okay," Darko shot back. "If you're gonna step aside

and let Jana make the connection to the beastmaster, then I'm going after Evilenko."

"You can't go up against Evilenko," Steve admonished him. "You can't win."

"You're not giving me a choice, Steve."

"You've been sticking your nose into my business, so let's try the shoe on the other foot. All you got on Evilenko is hearsay and rumors. There are no witnesses to anything he did back in Serbia, every one of them is dead. There are no indictments, no warrants for him. If he's here with that kind of money in his pocket, he's getting it from a big supporter, most likely the Chinese or the Russians. Look, why do you think I moved out of Soho to rent a room on Skid Row? I knew these guys wanted to talk to me, and I'm trying to lay low until I find out why. I appreciate you giving me the heads-up about Jana, but this is between me and whoever's looking for me. If it's Evilenko, then I'll meet up with him on my own terms and timeframe. You've got no business here. If you start butting in, the only one who'll get hurt is Jana."

"I think you're a pretty good guy who's got himself caught up in some bad business," Steve admitted. "If you recall, our last conversation was about placing you near those two dog killings. You're not exactly out of hot water yourself. Now I got Evilenko searching for you, and it doesn't look too good from where I'm sitting."

"What're you gonna do, Darko? Keep on harassing me, tailing Jana, and get out your slingshot and go after Evilenko?" Steve grew testy. "If I were in your shoes, I'd be out there trying to figure out why those dealers got killed instead of figuring out ways to work some dog trainers into your indictment. I'll tell you, it's gonna look pretty stupid when you've got a couple of Doberman Pinschers sitting up there on the witness stand. It'll look like something out of the *Trial of Lassie*, if you ask me."

"I'm gonna be looking at Evilenko," Lucic warned him as he got out of the car. "If you and Jana are in the way I'll be looking at the both of you too."

"Hey, it's the taxpayers' money," Steve shut the door behind him.

"Say, don't you want your coffee?" Tracker called after him, holding up the large bag of coffee and donuts as he returned to the vehicle.

"Give them to him," Steve waved him off, crossing the street. "He'll probably be up all night."

Both Steve and Darko knew that they would be seeing each other again very soon.

CHAPTER SIX

Darko Lucic felt as if he had most of the pieces of the puzzle before him, but he was having trouble making it all fit to see the big picture.

He felt as if the dog killings were just the tip of the iceberg here. He knew that he had nothing on Lurgan. There was no jury that would look crooked at a man who, as he clearly indicated, may have never owned a dog in his life. It was the whole Serbian thing that was jerking his own chain. Steve knowing Jana, who was suddenly hooked up with Evilenko by way of Ljubica, had a funny smell to it. He knew that Evilenko was the CEO of HPS, which was one of the major companies in the area where the runaway kids were murdered in the Catskills. The Catskill PD had put out a red alert throughout the vicinity and met with local business owners enlisting their help in the investigation. When he saw Evilenko's name on the reports, it was a red flag that made him think of Jana and Steve.

It was obvious that whoever had dissected those kids had a hidden medical facility somewhere in the New York area. It would make no sense for them to have abducted the kids in Manhattan, cut them open outside of the State, then ditched the bodies in upstate New York. It was a remote possibility that might have been designed to throw the authorities off, but Darko wasn't buying it. It was too much shuffling for a crew that was going away for a thousand years if they got caught red-handed.

The organ black market seemed to be a wave of the future, particularly in Third World countries where life was cheap and economies were in disastrous condition. There were reports of people from Delhi in India who had been kidnapped, drugged, and had their kidneys removed before they were tossed back onto the street. A black market ring in South Africa had been recruiting donors from the streets of Brazil, where people were paid ten grand for organs which were sold in Johannesburg for $100,000. There had also been a case involving Biomedical Tissue Services in New York, who was buying organs from local embalmers unknown to the families of the deceased. It was a good business, and with the increase in transplant research, it did not seem the demand would decrease anytime soon.

His research indicated that there had been a similar operation near the Sar Mountains in Kosovo during the Serbian War. Albanian insurgents had allegedly masterminded the operation, and hundreds of hostages taken during the fighting were rumored to have been killed for their organs up to the end of the war. It was rumored that the Chinese were the primary market for the operation, but once the war had ended there had been no trace found of any such ring, thus there was never an investigation.

He knew that Evilenko's nickname in Serbia was the Beast of the Black Mountains, but that was a way from the Accursed Mountains, which might have been more apropos. He got that nickname for annihilating Albanian rebels in the region and taking no prisoners in combat. There were rumors of him ordering the massacre of a number of hamlets in the area, but there were never survivors, and the attacks attributed to militant groups avenging murders perpetrated by Muslims against Serbian Christians.

Evilenko's alleged involvement with the Serbian White Knights was also of interest. They were a supremacist group dedicated to the preventive maintenance of the Serbian race and nation, its society and culture. If Evilenko was contributing to the group, they probably had a safe place for him to land if he ever had to flee America. They were probably also condoning whatever he was doing to put money on their table. It wouldn't change the nature of Evilenko but would give him extra leverage in earning the devotion of his followers.

That was where the interest in Steve Lurgan began to fit in. If Steve had witnessed the dog killings and knew who let the dogs out, then Evilenko was in excellent position to make contact and offer a deal with the assassins. It would make anyone less likely to offer information leading to the arrest of the kidnappers if they thought someone was going to put killer dogs on their ass in return. Darko was beginning to doubt that Steve had anything to do with it, but that did not mean that Evilenko felt the same.

Murder was murder, and the NYPD would track down anyone who took a human life. From where Darko sat, snatching kids off the street just because they ran off from home or just couldn't find a place to stay was just as bad as snatching them off campus. They had always taught all the way back in Academy that every human being was loved by someone, and therefore needed saving. When he thought of the families who had endured the grief of finding their children had been taken upstate and carved up for their organs, it made him sick.

He realized his only connection to Evilenko was Ljubica. He didn't want to place undue pressure on him because he could easily go into the wind, especially in light of the pending indictments of his Mob connections. Yet it was well known that Ljubica was a good earner, and he wouldn't take off and leave his customers to get swiped by a rival bookie or loan shark unless he had no choice. He would have to turn Ljubica over somehow, and the trick would be to put something extra on the hook beside advance warning that the Russians were about to fry.

Lucic and Tracker drove out to Chinatown and confronted Ljubica, who said he had some information in exchange for immunity in any prosecution of the Russian Mob. He told them he would meet with them at a rendezvous point at midnight so as not to be seen with the cops by his associates. Lucic readily agreed, realizing that this might finally be the big break that could help him solve this case and get him a nice desk job far away from the stink of the streets at last.

Jana Dragana had returned to her apartment to pack, and she wrote out a letter to Steve Lurgan as an afterthought. She was concerned for his well-being and hoped that things were going well for him out in California. She started realizing that she really did care for him, and she had found herself physically attracted to him from the moment they first met. After getting to know him, she found that he was a sensitive, intelligent man, the kind she always hoped she would meet and become involved with one day. He told her he had a well-paying profession, and she had no doubt of that considering the kind of rent they were paying, and the fact that he had not worked regularly since she met him. She knew he went out on assignments now and again, and it seemed to be the kind of work schedule that was both lucrative and comfortable.

She had her own vision quest and imagined her on the cover of international magazines one day, but was not opposed to have someone special in her life awaiting her at the end of the rainbow. She had avoided getting into a relationship back in Europe, because she knew some macho instinct would transform most hunks into hair-pulling troglodytes when the notion of leaving the country in pursuit of fame and fortune was introduced. When she came to America, she realized it would be more of a manipulation process where the dominant male would go behind her back and sever her connections to force her into docility. Steve, she believed, was not that kind of guy.

She slipped the letter in an envelope under his door and was startled as Steve opened the door abruptly. She looked up at him defensively before they shared a laugh as he gave her a hand and pulled her to her feet.

"Well, hello, stranger. When did you get in?"

"A little while ago," he replied, stepping aside and beckoning her in. "I'm kinda going in and out. I have an assignment out by the Canadian border. I'm gonna be flying up to Niagara Falls, then over to Vancouver. I'd sure like you to come along if you had time."

"Why, that is very nice of you, Steve," she said tentatively, caught off-guard by the offer. "I was just in process of packing myself, that was the reason why I dropped off that note. I landed a job with a software research company in Catskill. I'm going to be working there during the week and coming home on weekends."

He offered to make coffee and she gratefully accepted, talking a seat on the couch as he headed into the kitchenette. He listened quietly as she told him all about her fruitless job searches on the Internet, and how she got a call out of the blue on a referral that led her to Zora Vlasic.

"Have you done any research on the company?" he wondered. "You know, just to make sure the company's solvent and that they're going to be able to pay you."

"Well, not just yet," she admitted softly. He could tell by her voice that she was going on the defensive, and that was not what he wanted.

"I just don't want to see you go all the way out there and be disappointed," he said, having loaded the coffeemaker and pushed the button to pour the boiling water. "You know, Jana, I've pretty well kept to myself for the last few years since I came back from Serbia. Maybe it has something to do with that post-traumatic stress disorder, I don't know. One thing, though, I haven't gotten close to too many people, and you're really one of the only friends I have. I guess what I'm trying to say is that I care a good deal about you and wouldn't want to see you hurt in any way."

"That---that's very nice of you to say that," Jana suddenly felt very self-conscious. "I---I guess I haven't made many friends myself here. You know, people in show business and the modeling industry are very superficial, and many of them can be hypocrites. Sure, you learn to play the game, but it doesn't mean I trust too many of them. I've kind of kept to myself as well, and I must admit I consider you one of my closest friends as well."

"I'm flattered that you think of me like that, and I hope I can continue being worthy of your trust and your friendship," he said at risk of sounding hokey. He had a hell of a lot more he wanted to say but did not dare to.

"I want you to trust me as well, Steve," she looked at him earnestly. "I know that you're a very private person, almost mysterious at times. I just want you to know that I'm always there for you, if there is anything you ever want to talk about, I am there. You spent a long time with my people, you know that we do not take friendships lightly. And I am always there to lend a hand. If there is anything I can do within my power, I would be ready to help any way I can."

"Well, I feel the same way, Jana," he replied as he poured their coffee.

He wanted to ask her point blank about her drug dependency, offer anything he could. He would move heaven and hell if there was a single thing that would change as a result. Most of all, he wanted to tell her that he loved her.

"Why don't you let me look these people up for you on the Internet?" he asked gently. "It wouldn't take very long, and you could be pretty sure there wouldn't be any surprises ahead."

"I guess so," she was reluctant. He knew that she did not want to appear foolish, and was probably more worried about being embarrassed if he did find something wrong just before she was headed to the Amtrak station.

He went over to his work station in the anteroom just off the living room area and logged on, doing a quick search after Jana went back to her apartment to retrieve the business card she had been given.

"Well, their website seems solid, and I did a few name checks and it looks like they're hooked up with quite a few other companies," Steve finally conceded after a cursory check. "I guess you don't have much choice but to go take a look. Now, you've got my cell phone number. Maybe I don't pick up here in town, but if I see your number this weekend on Caller ID, I'll be ready to come running."

"Okay, my dear friend," she gave him a big hug as he walked her to the door. "Say a prayer for me, and I'll call as soon as I get back if you are not here."

The feel of her body next to his gave him a sudden rush, and the scent of her hair was exhilarating. He patted her back softly, wanting more than anything to hold her in his arms just a little bit longer.

"You be careful, Jana," he smiled.

She closed the door softly, taking a little piece of his heart along with her.

Lucic and Tracker arrived at the waterfront under the Manhattan Bridge just before midnight where they had arranged to meet with Ilija Ljubica. Lucic noticed that Ljubica did not use a car to get around and probably relied on cabs, or perhaps rides from his Russian gang pals. On this night he was all alone on the street, standing near an ancient chain link fence surrounding a badly disrepaired private dock. The cops pulled up to where he was and got out of the car to meet him on the sidewalk away from a lone street light near the corner of the block.

"Some place you picked to do business," Lucic griped. "Don't you think a patrol car'd be over here in a minute, wondering what the hell we're doing out here?"

"It's still a free country to my knowledge," Ljubica countered. "Of course, with this Administration, who can tell."

"We're not here to discuss politics, Ilija. What do you have for me?"

"Fetisov sent me to make a deal with you," Ljubica revealed. "He's got word that Evilenko is planning to expand his operations into the Manhattan area. He's got

some big investors with the Russians and the Chinese.
Fetisov is worried that some of the *vors*[1] in Moscow may be
turning against him and backing Evilenko."

"What does he think I can do to help?"

"He thinks you're investigating Evilenko for those
kidnap victims whose bodies were found in the Catskills.
He's got evidence that you might be able to use. They just
want your personal assurance that if they give it over, you're
going to do what you can to get the Feds off his back. He
believes it is a fair trade, letting him slide in exchange for
the murderers of the missing children."

"He should know I don't have the authority to make
that kind of deal," Lucic shook his head. "I can talk to
Captain Willard, and he can see if Chief Madden will go
for it, but I can't give him a guarantee on anything."

"His underboss has come to meet you," Ljubica nodded
towards the abandoned building across the street. "Their
car comes to pick them up in fifteen minutes. This is a one-
time offer. If you are unwilling to intercede, they will act
without you and take on Evilenko themselves."

"Shit," Lucic hissed. He didn't think Ljubica would be
pulling anything stupid here. He knew how unpredictable
the Russians were, and they might be quick to perceive
Lucic's refusal as an insult. The bottom line was, if any of
this got out, it could be said by his detractors that Lucic let
an opportunity pass to prevent a gang war within the
Russian Mob.

"Right up there," Ljubica pointed to the darkened
doorway whose door was either broken down or missing.
"I'm going to walk up to Canal Street and catch a cab so
nobody will know I was anywhere near here."

The cops headed for the doorway and unclipped their
holsters, ready to draw at the first sign of trouble. The

musty-smelling hallway was crowded by a staircase leading to the upper floor. Lucic and Tracker approached on the balls of their feet, trudging carefully up the steps with eyes and ears wide open.

As they both came onto the landing, they saw that the entire showcase floor was deserted, the windows on each side of the huge room having long been broken out. They walked forth in search of the Russians, and suddenly men stepped out from behind the four large pillars that supported the roof. They opened fire with silencer-fitted pistols, riddling Benny Tracker with bullets as he fell to the dusty floor.

"Hands over your head!" the leader of the masked men came forth. "Make a dumb move and you die with your friend!"

"Up that ladder!" a second gunman yelled, pointing to a ladder leading to a hatchway to the roof. "There's guys up there waiting, if you do anything stupid they'll blow your brains out!"

Lucic numbly did as he was told, walking away from Tracker towards the ladder. He knew that these might be the last moments of his life, and all he could do was play his hand and see if he could force a break somewhere. He climbed the ladder slowly and carefully, striving to do nothing that would make them open up on him next.

As they said, there were three men on the rooftop awaiting him. One of them grabbed him by the back of the collar and shoved him to the edge of the roof. He looked down and saw that the building sat atop a dock on a bay area leading directly into the river. The tallest of the masked men came over and stood just behind Lucic.

"This is it, Detective," Bojan Evilenko said as his henchman faced Lucic towards the edge of the roof. "This is your payoff for your dedication, your bravery, your tenac-ity...and your uncompromising stupidity."

Lucic heard the hammer of the revolver click and threw himself forward. He heard the gunman fire and felt a couple of grazing shots burning his back before he plum-meted over two hundred feet into the East River.

CHAPTER SEVEN

Vagrants seeking refuge under the bridges and inside the abandoned warehouses around the area notified locals who called police. They found the unconscious detective on the loading dock at the break of dawn. Lucic was rushed to Bellevue Hospital while police vessels were summoned to fish Benny Tracker's body out of the river. He had left behind a wife and five kids, and the entire city was stunned by the tragic loss.

Lucic told the investigating officers at the hospital that it was Ilija Ljubica who had directed him and Benny into the warehouse, but he did not want Ljubica picked up just yet. He told them he wasn't sure if Ljubica had anything to do with it. Most likely he was just following orders. He told them the gunmen all wore masks and gave no reason why they had lured the cops to their doom.

The bullets had hit his left bicep and his right buttock. The one that had done the serious damage lodged in his spine and would require surgery to remove. For now, it was in such an area that they would not tamper with it lest a failed attempt crippled him for life. The hospital provided him with a wheelchair and crutches before letting him out the next morning.

He got a call from Steve Lurgan, who was waiting for him at the emergency entrance with a panel truck. Steve and one of the attendants helped Darko into the passenger seat before folding up the wheelchair and depositing it in the back of the truck.

"Hope you've still got control of your plumbing or we're gonna have problems," Steve quipped as they headed back to Lucic's apartment in Greenwich Village.

"Nah, everything's working except my back. They loaded me up with hydrocodone. If I shift wrong, it's like Con Edison flips a switch on me. Electric shocks go off all over from the chest down. They say they're gonna have to let my spine set itself around the bullet before they try and pull it out. Too soon, it'll cause more damage. Too late and it'll be there forever."

They arrived at Lucic's place and went through the hassle of loading Darko onto the wheelchair and rolling him into the building on West 4th Street. They took the elevator to his third floor apartment, where Steve helped him get situated in his recliner before looking about for the makings for a pot of coffee.

"Okay, here's my offer," Steve brought the coffee in and took a seat on the sofa in the living room across from Lucic. "I'll give you the dog handlers in exchange for your help in rescuing Jana. Somehow Bojan Evilenko found out I was here in the City and thought I had a lead on the black-market organ harvesters. He knew I had been investigating them back in Kosovo during the war. He made a connection with Jana and lured her up there, then he sent me an e-mail making me a job offer. I'm positive that if I don't agree, he'll threaten Jana to force me to go it with him."

"Shit," Lucic stared at the carpet. "I can't believe this. I'll bet Evilenko had something to do with ambushing me and Benny. He probably wanted to get us out of the way if he suspected we were looking you. I'm not ruling out Ilija Ljubica either. We leaned on him for information about Evilenko. I'll tell you, though, if Evilenko's in with the Russian Mob he's got some serious weight behind him. Those guys are getting as strong as the Mafia here in the City."

"What we need is a safe room, an underground vault or a meat locker somewhere," Steve suggested. "I'll make an arrangement so that you can find out everything you need to know about the dog handlers. After that, I need your solemn promise that you'll help me rescue Jana."

"Safe room? Vault?"

"It's got to be something that happens right away, Darko. Time's a major factor here. I can't afford to sit around and wait for you to set this up."

"Okay, relax," Darko held up his hand. "There's a drug dealer out on Staten Island we took down a week or so ago on a RICO charge. The Government grabbed everything in the place and locked it down. The guy had an underground vault where he kept all his stuff: money, drugs and guns. When he got busted it turned into an evidence room. I know the crew watching the place, they can get me the keys."

"All right," Steve agreed softly. "You give me a call when you get everything set up and I'll be back about five PM."

"Sounds like a plan," Lucic agreed.

Darko spent the morning on the phone and finally called Steve to tell him everything was set. An NYPD patrol car came out late that afternoon to drop off the keys to the mansion, and Steve showed up about a half hour later. They went through the labor of loading Darko onto the wheelchair and into the van outside, and soon they were on their way downtown towards the Staten Island Ferry. Darko noticed that Steve kept looking at his watch and figured he must have made a dead-on appointment with the dog people. He had given Steve the address in advance, so doubtlessly the handlers would be waiting for them.

He rolled down the window as they cruised across the river to the Island, breathing in the salt water as the ferry chugged along. He felt a wave of nostalgia as he thought back to his childhood days when his mother would bring him down here sightseeing. He was in middle school when they fled Serbia, and she was intent on learning everything about their new homeland and taking her with him on her excursions. She was determined that they assimilated their new culture, but he found that it was impossible to put Serbia behind him completely, Never did that realization appear more certain than now.

They drove from the ferry station along the roads into the residential areas, and found the dealer's mansion surrounded by an eight-foot wall with a wrought iron main gate. Darko gave Steve the keys, and he unlocked the padlocked chain so he could bring the van through before locking up behind them. He then went through the process of unloading Darko onto the wheelchair before opening up the thick wooden doors of the stuccoed mansion to permit them entry. Steve brought a heavy canvas bag with him as he wheeled Darko inside.

"So where are your guys supposed to meet us, are they gonna call you?"

"Well, first things first. Where's the vault?"

They took the mansion's elevator to the basement level,

and Steve wheeled Darko to the west end of the chamber where the massive vault door was located. It was as if inside a bank, and Darko had to give Steve a set of codes to open the steel enclosure. There was also a red emergency button on the panel, and that could be activated to open the vault without the code should someone be trapped inside by accident.

"Fine and dandy," Steve exhaled tautly, noticing the monitor set at a console near the vault providing visual access by way of a camera set inside. It allowed for the owner to see activity inside the vault without having to open it in the event that someone managed to get inside undetected. "This should work just fine. I'm going to need you to tape this whole thing. Do you know how to work this stuff?"

"I've been a cop for about twenty years," Darko retorted. "Look, I think you'd better let me in on what's happening here. When do your boys show up?"

"All right, I'll level with you, and some of it's gonna be very hard to swallow until everything starts happening," Steve checked his watch again. "No one's coming out, it's just you and me."

"You gotta be kidding," Darko was exasperated.

"Back in the Nineties, when I was in Kosovo, I contracted this disease called lycanthropia," Steve tried to explain. "It's an extremely rare condition and there's no known cure. I'm pretty sure that Evilenko was fascinated by its possible military applications and started tracking me down. He traced me here in the States, and now he's trying to coerce me to help me with his project in some sick way."

"Lycanthropia?" Darko tried to laugh. "You mean like in the movies?"

"It's called clinical lycanthropy in psychiatric terms,"

Steve insisted. "The victim imagines himself transformed into a wolf. During the episodes, many people's hallucinations are so intense that they get supercharged on adrenaline and are capable of feats of superhuman strength. I'm sure you're familiar with PCP users going berserk and snapping handcuffs."

"So you want me to tape this," Darko exhaled tautly. "Look, I don't mind trying to help you, and I gave you my word to help Jana, but this isn't working too well on my end. I had corpses in the morgue that got torn up by dogs, or a real live wolf, not some guy imagining that he turned into one. I hope you're not going to renege on me with this."

"Look, just lock me in that vault, turn the video on, and no matter what happens, for god's sake, don't open that door. Understand?" Steve stared frantically at his watch, knowing that the sun had probably set and the full moon outside would be visible in the night sky.

"Okay, but there's only gonna be enough air in there to last you until morning," Darko rolled himself over to where Steve swung open the vault and switched on the fluorescent lighting.

"That'll be more than enough time," Steve said as he entered the vault and closed the massive door behind him.

It was the crack of dawn by the time Darko finally opened the vault door. It was the most horrific night he had ever experienced, and between Benny being murdered and him put into a wheelchair, these past seventy-two hours had been as hell on earth for him. He was still doubting his sanity and wondered whether the stress had put him over the edge.

"Steve!" he called into the vault. "Steve!"

Lurgan laid naked face down on the metal floor, his clothes and boots ripped to shreds, laying tattered all around him. Darko was astonished that not only Steve was without a scratch, but there was not a drop of blood to be seen anywhere. Steve managed to raise his head and roll over, summoning his strength so that he could rise to his feet and walk out of the vault.

"Did you tape it?" Steve went to the canvas bag and retrieved a spare set of clothes.

"Yeah, I taped it," Darko's mind was racing.

"I've never seen it before. I had to see the thing myself to figure out what to do with the rest of my life."

"The screams were the most terrible thing," Darko said as he stared unseeingly at the dark screen. "It was not the scream of one man or beast. It was the tortured cry of dozens of souls, maybe hundreds, possibly thousands. I believe they are still trapped inside the beast. I believe they are all within him, screaming from the abyss, all those who he has possessed. I heard their cries all night, and I pray to God that I will never hear them again."

Steve flipped on the switch and ran the time back to 1800 hours, seeing where he stepped into the vault from an overhead view in the corner as the sequence began.

"If it wasn't the screams, it was the cries of the tortured animal," Darko stared numbly at the ceiling. "I've loved animals all my life, and the way that thing screamed, my god, it was unbearable. It sounded like it was getting butchered. And when it wasn't screaming or crying, it was roaring, like some monster from hell, the Devil himself. They haven't made a movie that could make that noise. I can't even describe it, it was a roar of raw hatred, fury, evil. I don't know how in hell anything that could roar like that wasn't able to come right through that door."

"Holy crap," Steve stared at the monitor in awed reverence. "Holy crap."

"Steve, I've used up my entire bottle of hydrocodone. I should be stoned out of my head, but I'm perfectly awake. My mind is flying like a rocket, but my body feels like I got caught in an avalanche. I gotta get back to my house, or the hospital, anywhere but here."

"Oh my god," tears spilled down Steve's cheeks as he saw what had possessed him for almost fifteen years. "Oh my god."

"I don't know how this is gonna go down, Steve," Darko managed. "How can you take that thing anywhere? How are you gonna control it? How do you know it won't kill Jana, or me? Even worse, how are you gonna set something like that on another human being?"

"If Evilenko gets control of it, you'll see a wave of terror in this City like you couldn't imagine, and you know it," Steve muttered.

He watched the video as his body convulsed, being tossed to the ground by the demon before he went into violent spasms and contortions. He saw himself curl into a fetal position and lay there for a long while before eventually the head of the wolf rose and peered over his shoulder. It began preening itself, ripping and tearing the clothes from its body until it finally stood and shook itself off. It then began snarling and growling, sniffing around the thirty-foot vault before realizing it was locked in. It then began howling and roaring, slamming against the door to no avail. Steve fast-forwarded it an hour ahead, at which point it began smashing itself against the door until its muzzle was dripping with blood and foam.

At that point it began chewing its own paws up, ripping itself as if trying to escape from a trap. It gnawed itself to the bone until if could no longer stand up, then fell to one side and lay crying until suddenly going after its back legs. It began chewing its hind paws until it laid in a pool of its own blood. At that point, the crippled animal laid on its side, crying, screaming and roaring on into the night. Steve fast-forwarded it again up to 0600 hours, and the animal had curled into a fetal position and laid there until Darko opened the vault. Steve rewound and fast-forwarded, and could only perceive that the beast's blood had seemingly evaporated as water.

"If you're gonna run it again, you're gonna have to kill the volume," Darko mumbled.

"No, I've seen enough. Go ahead and erase it, and let's go."

They drove in silence back to the ferry, but as the boat began the cruise across the river, Steve suddenly became animated by what he had seen.

"You know, it was like being alcohol intolerant at first," he revealed. "I'd black out and couldn't remember anything. Over the years, I got to where I could remember snippets of things, like in a dream. This is the first time I've seen it happen, and now it makes more sense. The damn thing's invulnerable. I know it's taken bullets before, it's survived automatic fire. Did you hear how it banged on that vault door? The steel door was echoing from the pounding. Plus, the way it survived after chewing itself up. Darko, if there was a way it could be used for good, think of it. The damn thing might help find a cure for cancer."

"I don't know what you're gonna do with this," Darko was still overwhelmed by the experience. "I don't know how anyone will be able to get a grip on this thing. We shouldn't have erased the tape. No one in their right minds will believe us."

"I couldn't take a chance of you turning on me, Darko," Steve revealed. "Lots of guys would've kept me locked up and called the cops. I took a big chance by letting you in on this. My only hope would've been the cops blowing you off and putting me away for observation. I trusted you because I need your help. I'm still gonna need you to help me rescue Jana."

"Steve, I still gotta wrap my head around this whole thing," Darko admitted. "How can I let you loose this thing on Evilenko? I'd be an accessory to murder, at the very least. If that thing did what it did to those drug dealers, what in hell else is it capable of?"

"Look, Jana's life is in danger. If you back down, and even if you called the cops and warned Evilenko, he'd just move Jana to where I couldn't find her. Even if you put a bullet in my head right now and ended this thing, you still let Jana die. She's seen too much by now for Evilenko taking a chance on letting her live. He just had your partner killed, he just murdered a cop. Do you think there's anything he won't do to get to where he's going?"

"We gotta let somebody else in on this," Darko insisted. "It's gotten too big for us. Suppose something happens to me, or suppose he gets hold of you and learns the secret? Suppose there's a way he can analyze your blood and find a way to reproduce that thing? He doesn't need you anymore, he can knock you off and turn his own people into monsters."

"Look, there's a lot more to it, it's not that easy. I got infected by someone else who had the disease. They attacked me and I killed them, and the thing took possession of me, like a demonic possession. It's not in my blood, it's in my head. You've seen that *Exorcist* stuff, it's not just superstition, they've got documented proof that things like this happen."

"Not like this, Steve. Not like this."

"All right, listen. If you help me rescue Jana, I'll move away somewhere, out of the country, and no one'll ever see me again. Now that I've seen the damn thing, I know there's no other way. We'll get her out any way we can, maybe I can find her and just walk her out without a problem. Evilenko's running a legitimate front, I don't know that he'll want to make a move on me in broad daylight. If I can get her out without a scene, we'll be okay. I'm not going to wait until dark unless it's the only way."

"You gonna drop me off?" Darko relented.

"I'll be back around two, it should take us a few hours to drive upstate," he replied. "I'm going to try and get Jana's e-mail or send her a text on her cell phone. I'm gonna let her know everything I can about Evilenko's company and hopefully have her ready to go by the time we get there."

"Okay, I'll go one more round," Darko exhaled tautly. "They killed my partner and put me in a wheelchair. I know this is something I may regret for the rest of my life, but I agree that there's an innocent girl caught in the middle of this. I warn you, my friend, if any innocent civilians get caught in the middle of this, I get on my cell phone and I call the SWAT team."

"I wouldn't have it any other way."

And so the two men continued on to their date with destiny.

CHAPTER EIGHT

Jana had gotten the e-mail from Steve just before 4 PM that afternoon. It contained a .zip file and told her to use the software to learn more about the Company and why she should make plans to leave immediately. She opened the file and found instructions to access Safecracker ver. 78.9. She did so reluctantly, and a Mr. Peanut-type character winked through his monocle, tipping his top hat before using his walking stick as the cursor. He walked her through the tutorial and at once she had a icon on her desk in the right upper-hand corner of her screen that appeared only when she passed her cursor over it.

"Jana, I will be on premises until late this evening, but I will be incommunicado," Evilenko's voice came in over the intercom. "If anything comes up, contact Ilija on his cell phone. He and the men will be on hand to supervise a large delivery of equipment this evening. I understand you will be here until about nine. You can let yourself out the front gate. If there are guards posted, they will let you out themselves."

"Thank you, Mr. Vlasic," she cooed.

This was one of the worst situations she had ever been involved in. Mr. Vlasic treated her like a daughter, and Ilija Ljubica had almost been as a trusted friend over the past couple of days. She checked her bank account, and $7,692 had been deposited the morning she arrived at MPS to report for work. She paid off her credit card balance and most of her bills in one fell swoop, and was eager to get started. They gave her a training manual that walked her through her very small list of duties. Most of what she did was keep Mr. Vlasic's appointment schedule in order, and checked on the guards to make sure they were maintaining their hourly patrol.

Compromising this situation was making her tummy churn. If they found out she was hacking on them, she would be fired for sure. Since she was using a company car to get back and forth to her rented suite, she might even have to walk back to town. She would have blown Steve off entirely if they had not also expressed a strong desire to have him join their staff. He must have come up with some urgent information about wrongdoing by HPS to have suggested that she endanger her position thusly. It was only her belief in what kind of person Steve was, and knowing how he cared for her, that encouraged her to proceed.

She opened the file, and Poindexter from *Felix the Cat* next appeared in the small screen, which only appeared when touched by her cursor. He directed her to pull up the Company's restricted account database, and asked her to wait as he began translating the names of the file folders. He then pointed out that an encrypted file named "China" appeared to be the most secure database, and asked her if she wished to proceed.

Poindexter next located the China file folders and translated the names of the files, then indicated he would be ready to convert the text and graphics of each file she chose to look into. She clicked the Donor file, and it pulled up a list that appeared as if they were patients in a medical file. By double-clicking, she found detailed medical information, and yet another option allowed her to view their autopsy report. With trembling fingers she chose the final prompt, showing what organs they had donated and which remained available.

Beyond the shadow of a doubt, the Company was involved with far more than software research. She had read about the kidnappings of runaways in New York City, and their butchered remains found in upstate New York, but dismissed the articles as tabloid fanfare. She was familiar with such rumors all the way back in Serbia, where militants had accused the Muslims of doing the same thing. Many dismissed this as propaganda meant to demonize the enemy, but in this case the evidence came from the perpetrators' own documents.

Still refusing to believe her eyes, she did a Google search for the patients listed in the database. She found one, then another, and was horrified by the discovery that each patient was listed as a missing person by the NYPD. She was now faced with the prospect of having to notify the police of her discovery. Either that, or she would have to confront Mr. Vlasic with her findings. That could possibly be a fatal error on her part, as people involved in this kind of business were connected to murderers who would undoubtedly kill to cover their tracks.

She frantically considered her options, and was nowhere near a solution when two figures appeared at the threshold of the enormous suite where Jana had her own side office cubicle. She looked up and saw Zora Vladic walk in with Ilija Ljubica accompanying him.

"Jana, my dear," Evilenko smiled curtly. "You seem a bit under the weather."

"Yes, Mr. Vladic," she winced. "I've got this headache that won't go away."

"It seems to have come upon you quite suddenly. You seemed quite well a short while ago. Nevertheless, I do know how such things can creep up out of nowhere. We just have no way of knowing how a crisis can develop at a moment's notice, do we?"

"I---guess not, sir," Jana cleared her throat, cupping her face in her hands momentarily to try and sort herself out.

"Why don't you go ahead and take the rest of the day off, my dear," he smiled softly. "It's after regular hours anyway. Ilija will escort you to your vehicle so you don't have to deal with those pesky security guards all over the grounds. They are bringing in some important equipment and are IDing everyone to discourage corporate spying by unauthorized persons on the grounds."

"Thank you very much sir, I do apologize. I'll be right on time tomorrow, for sure."

"Have a good evening, Jana. Do get some rest."

There was an uncomfortable silence between her and Ilija as they rode the elevator down to the sub-basement garage level, and she found the black Mitsubishi Galant alone in the lot at this time of evening as usual. They bade each other a good evening, but as she gunned the engine she found it had gone dead.

"Tsk, tsk, these Japanese cars," Ilija stood at a distance, shaking his head. Somehow she got a weird feeling that he was anticipating such an event. He told her that he would have the dealer send a replacement immediately, and that he would have her wait in one of the break rooms downstairs while he did so.

He held the door for her, and she stepped into the room where a couple of tables were sat alongside one another amidst snack machines on each side. She sighed as she rummaged through her purse, pulling out her cell phone and finding she could not get a signal down here. As an afterthought, she decided to go to the restroom to touch up, and was startled to find the door was locked.

She grew panicked as she began calling out and pounding on the thick, narrow window panel of the steel door. She looked as far as she could to either side and saw the floor deserted. She realized her only hope was for Ilija to return, and resignedly took a seat at the table hoping he returned before she worked herself into a panic attack.

Outside, Steve and Darko had pulled up in the van just as the sun began setting in the west. It filled the sky with angry splotches of red, gold and purple before giving place to the silvery moon, and the two men stared at it in trepidation as they prepared for the worst.

They had watched the four black panel trucks pull up with their gold HPS logos on the side, the powerfully-built stern-faced men unloading what appeared to be specially-constructed steel chests from the vehicles. Both Steve and Darko guessed that these were the transport containers for the organs and body parts, which were either being delivered for shipping or waiting to be packed. They were both appalled by the thought of so many organs having been harvested, and that business was so brisk that the parts of the dissected were just waiting to be received and purchased by eager buyers.

"Okay," Steve grunted painfully, "It's happening. As soon as the change is completed, pop that door and stay away from the window. The damned thing should be able to let itself out."

A thrill of dread coursed along Darko's spine as Steve launched himself out the door and climbed into the back of the van. He had seen the change take place on the video but had no idea what it would be like going on alongside him with just a thin metal wall separating him from the beast. He also knew that the damned thing was probably about three hundred pounds and stood over six feet tall on its hind legs. This would be like having a pro football player wanting to rip one's head off, if ever the player had the strength of a demon-possessed animal. At once he repented of ever having agreed to such a thing. The concept of saving lives suddenly hit him flush in the face, and he was about to confront Steve and call it off before the wolf began to cry.

It was the most horrific sound he had ever heard, the screams and cries of dozens of men trapped inside the beast, begging to be released from the living hell that had become Steve's body. They screamed and pleaded in a cacophony of tortured voices until they eventually blended into a primal roar, worse than any cat, ape or dog ever created. He heard the pounding of Steve's thrashing limbs turn into a thumping and scratching, and it was as if Darko was being allowed to hear the transmogrification of his arms and legs taking place.

He did not once dare to look through the window. He remained frozen in the driver's seat, hoping that the monster would not know he was there in simply wanting to escape. Darko popped the door locks and sat transfixed as the roars abated, the wolf trying to get its bearings. It was silent for an eternal moment, before suddenly the abomination realized the doors could be forced open. The doors were slammed as if to be ripped from their hinges, and the van bounced as the three hundred-pound weight sprang away in a flash.

Both Evilenko and Ljubica were in the executive suite on the second floor, observing everything in the facility and the surrounding area on their state of the art surveillance system. They saw the beast leap over the guardrail at the main gate and charge across the field like a small horse. They were astounded as the monster pounced onto the loading dock and began ripping into the crowd of over a dozen men. Although shots were fired, no one under heaven could have prepared themselves for such an onslaught, and so they tried to flee but were brought down from behind and torn to pieces.

"Here," Evilenko went to a wall panel hidden behind an oil painting, and pulled it open to reveal a cache of automatic weapons. He produced an AK-47 automatic rifle mounted with an under-barrel BGA-40 grenade launcher, handing it to Ljubica. "This will stop the creature in its tracks. I will meet you at the rendezvous in Brooklyn where we will launch our alternative plan. Undoubtedly Lucic will have this place crawling with cops within hours. You can leave the girl or finish her off, it makes no difference at this point."

"How---" Ljubica's mind raced as he took the weapon from Evilenko. He knew that the Captain had planned to proposition Lurgan into joining the organization as an enforcer and assassin, but the details were never discussed. There was no way anyone could have thought of such a thing as this. There were no words to describe the carnage that he had just witnessed on the monitor. Even though he was a seasoned veteran with twenty years of battle experience, he felt almost as if he was being handed a bow and arrow in going against a lion.

"I don't care what it is, it cannot stand against a grenade," Evilenko snarled. "Lock the elevator up and do not step off until you clearly see the damned thing. Shoot it down as you will, but if you have the range, fire the grenade and finish it off. We'll never return here, we have no further use for this place. Blow it to hell if you have to, and we will meet in Brooklyn tomorrow."

Ljubica watched as Evilenko disappeared in the shadows in the rear of the suite. He knew that the Captain must have had his own escape tunnel prepared with a vehicle awaiting him in an emergency. He could not believe how such a lucrative operation such as this could collapse so suddenly, and he refused to believe it was through the efforts of a low-level gumshoe like Lucic. He surmised that it somehow had to do with Lurgan, and once he blew up Steve's damned animal he was going to go looking for him next. He would probably put a bullet in Jana for good measure to ensure that she had no tales to carry.

He rode the elevator to the basement level, and put the key in the control panel to allow him to adjust the sliding door from inside. He allowed the door to slide halfway open, then about three quarters after that. Apparently the girl had heard the elevator arrive, as she was banging and yelling with vigor to get someone's attention. He smiled as he thought of all the attention she would get as soon as this damned animal was put down.

The hair on his nape rose with dread as he saw the great beast slowly descending the vehicle ramp from the upper level, its glowing red eyes staring directly at Ljubica across the parking area from fifty yards away. Its muzzle, chest and front legs were caked with blood and gore, and it seemed as if traces of entrails were hanging from its jowls. It began stalking Ljubica, creeping in his direction before breaking into a run. Ilija cocked the grenade launcher, then deliberately aimed and fired at the beast. Ljubica was astonished as the monster nimbly hopped to the side, the grenade soaring past the wolf and exploding against the rampway behind it. With that, the beast was as a streak of light as it covered the ground to the elevator and roared in at Ljubica. He began emptying the clip of the AK-47 at the creature, but it smashed him against the wall of the elevator before he had time to pivot.

Jana stared frantically out the narrow window of the locked door, and could only see the flash of the explosion before the air was filled with smoke and concrete dust. She wiped the glass to no avail, and could hear the screams of Ljubica that soon faded under the crashing sounds of metal from the elevator. She quaked with terror as she backed away from the door, hearing the sound of clicking as something terrible deliberately approached.

She screamed as the thick glass suddenly exploded as what appeared to be a pair of claws came through the narrow window and began yanking at it with incredible ferocity. The metal appeared to buckle under the force until, at once, the door frame gave way and the door crashed against the outside wall, giving way to a terrifying silence. Jana sobbed uncontrollably, not daring to step forth in stark fear of the thing that lurked outside.

Long minutes passed before she was able to force herself to walk towards the doorway. There was no other way out of here, and if the monster had left, she would at least be able to run up the ramp to the grade level and flee the premises. She crept towards the door and heard nothing outside. She wiped the tears from her eyes and made her way out into the lower level, nearly gagging from the concrete dust in the air. Suddenly she detected a presence, feeling it more than hearing it, then turned to her right and beheld the monster.

Jana Dragana tried to scream, but every bit of energy in her body was trapped in her throat. She stared at the beast before her, its head nearly reaching as high as her shoulders as it stood on all fours. Its serpentine eyes, shining as rubies, seemed as if to stare back into the depths of her very soul. She saw his fangs as it panted, its muzzle caked with blood. Every nerve in her body had switched into survival mode, and she was set to run for her life were it not for the terror gripping her heart. She realized that if she moved one inch, this monster would be able to rip her face off with one bite.

"Nice dog," she managed, the words just tumbling out of her mouth.

It narrowed its eyes, and she knew beyond doubt that she was dead. She began whispering prayers to Jesus, Mary and Joseph, but at once the wolf turned and galloped towards the exit ramp. She dropped to her knees, oblivious to the excruciating impact that would normally have caused her to scream with pain. The animal streaked up the ramp and disappeared.

All she was able to do was fall forward onto her face, sobbing hysterically in abject terror. She laid there and cried for a long, long time, then managed to rise to her feet to try and figure out a way to escape.

What she had considered Heaven just this morning had now become Hell.

CHAPTER NINE

Steve Lurgan woke up the next morning near a sewer pipe set inside a gully. He was stark naked, and rolled out from under some bushes to the opening where he found the trash bag he had set there. He quickly pulled on the clothes and retrieved his belongings, smiling wryly at the thought of a vagrant coming across the bag only to come face-to-face with the wolf. He shoved his wallet into his pocket, put on his Rolex watch, then called Darko Lucic on his cell phone.

"Steve," he answered. "I found Jana outside the complex and brought her back to the City. She's back at her place, I hope she's sleeping it off. I told her about everything but the wolf, and she agreed to stay put until she heard from us."

"You mean you left her at the apartment by herself?"

"I'm outside the apartment. I've been pissing in a can for twelve hours and I feel like I'm sitting in a can of hot coals. If Evilenko sends anyone after her I'll tail them as far as I can before I gotta call backup. Are you on your way back in?"

"As soon as I can get to the Amtrak station," he replied.

He next got on the Internet with his Smart Phone and located a car service near the area, summoning a vehicle to pick him up on the road in front of the HPS complex. The campus was absolutely serene form the outside, and no one would have any idea of the carnage inside until either he or Darko called the state police. While he awaited the car, he decided to call Jana.

"Hello?" she answered drowsily after six rings, then suddenly snapped. "Steve!"

"Jana. Are you okay?"

"Where are you?"

"I'm still in Catskill. Darko's downstairs in the van watching the front entrance. If Evilenko or any of his people show up he'll have backup there in minutes. I should be there in a few hours, so just sit tight."

"You mean no one's called the police yet? What about all those people who were killed by that monster, that wolf?"

"Jana, you saw that database. They were transporting body parts. The most important thing right now is catching Evilenko. He's got connections with the Russians and the Chinese, and if he leaves the country he'll never be brought to justice. If he thinks he's still got time, he'll probably make another move or two to close his business deals, and we'll be able to catch him."

"It was the second time I saw that animal, the second time it ripped people apart!" she began weeping. "How can something like this be happening! The only way I'll be able to convince anyone I'm not crazy is for them to find those bodies at the facility!"

"We've got proof that the wolf did what it did, and both Lucic and I can testify that we've seen it," he gently reassured her. "Plus I'm sure Evilenko's security cameras caught everything that happened on the loading dock. You don't have anything to worry about. Once we nail Evilenko, it'll all be over. Darko and I will make sure that you never see the animal again."

"How could such a thing happen!" she cried. "First Kane North and his friends were murdered, then Zora Vladic's employees! Someone is following me with that beast somehow! How could someone bring such a thing into my life, and why?"

"Jana, I've got a call coming in from Darko," he told her as his phone began beeping. "Let me see what he wants and I'll call you right back."

"Steve?" Lucic was anxious. "A car just pulled up and two men headed for the building. I've got a feeling they're Evilenko's."

"What're we gonna do?" Steve asked excitedly. "There's no other way out but through the front entrance. There's a way out into the back alley but there's no way onto the street from there. Are you gonna be able to tail them?"

"I'll do my best. If I lose them I got no choice but to call for backup."

"Keep me in the loop. I'll be there as soon as I can."

Steve was beside himself by the time the cabbie arrived, and he had the driver bring him to the car rental service in town instead. He picked out a Chevy Camaro and had the car streaking towards the highway within the hour. He knew it was a two and a half hour drive, and if he hauled ass he should be in town by nine AM at the latest. He figured that Darko would be able to stay on the Russians or whoever was after Jana, and if not, then at least the cops would come in and nail the bastards.

He knew that the end of the tribulation had come for him at last. No matter how it turned out, he was going to some place like Alaska or Arizona where he could let the beast run free in the wilderness a few days each month. There was no way he could have a true relationship with anyone, and he had been deceiving himself into thinking something was possible with Jana. The monster would be with him for the rest of his days. His only hope would be to get a shack in some secluded corner of the map and do the best he could until his time of the month came around, like some kind of freakish menstruation demanding the blood-letting of others.

He knew now that the monster was benevolent in its own screwed-up way, or it would have torn Jana apart. It was almost as if he remembered it staring at Jana, reveling in her horror before running away, even though he could not tell if it had been a dream or not. He remembered the crunching of bones and the tearing of flesh, huge chunks of flesh from men's forearms and legs. He also remembered that they had descended upon the wolf as if it were a large insect, a horrible thing that had to be crushed. How much of it was about a bestial killing spree, and how much was about survival? Certainly he had planned to have the beast walk in on them at the loading dock, but would there have been any bloodshed if they had just walked or ran away? If he could only remember. *God, if he could only remember.*

He sped down the I-87 back to the City, barely braking to avoid speed traps as the Highway Patrol sat in their cross-over lanes awaiting the careless. He thought they had him dead to rights at 80 MPH at one point, but swooped in and nailed a college student sailing back to the City instead. He used his tried-and-true method of playing leapfrog with other cars, closing in on them from behind little by little until breaking into a 90 MPH spurt to surpass them. He then crept up on the next car ahead and repeated the process.

"Steve," he switched on his phone as Darko called back. "They came out and they had Jana with them. It looks like they're driving into Brooklyn. They're going into rush hour so I don't think it's gonna be a problem staying on them. Let me know when you get into town and I'll tell you where we're at. Right now it looks like they're heading for the Manhattan Bridge, so just keep in touch. I'll let you go so I don't let my battery run low."

"Got it," Steve replied.

He chafed at having to pay a ten dollar toll for the privilege of being swallowed up into NYC's traffic congestion. He cruised into the torrent of honking vehicles trying to slip past each other en route to the Lincoln Tunnel and on to the Manhattan Bridge. He was amused by the notion of the wolf manifesting itself and bounding over the roofs of the vehicles to get to where it needed to be. Most likely there would be a whole lot of abandoned cars needing towing afterwards.

It was almost 9:30 by the time he hit the Manhattan Bridge, and dialed Darko to let him know.

"Okay, it looks like we're heading towards Flatlands in Flatbush, the warehouse area," Lucic reported. "I'm getting a low battery signal now. I'll get an address, find a place to stake them out, and call you back."

Steve got off the bridge and headed straight down Flatbush Avenue, driving much more casually now that he knew Darko had them pinpointed. He knew now that it was all about Evilenko trapping him and getting the secret of the wolf from him. He knew that Evilenko would use him as a guinea pig, experiment on him until he was able to harness the wolf's power. This was going to be a straight trade, giving himself up for Jana. He had only to make sure that Jana was safe before he agreed to Evilenko's terms, and that the beast could free itself when the sun went down once more.

"And so you see, my dear, Steve Lurgan somehow managed to have the beast transported here to the United States, and was planning to offer his services to the highest bidder," Evilenko said kindly to the weeping girl across the desk from him in his tastefully-furnished office. "He had made connections with the blackmarket traffickers in Kosovo during the war, and somehow took possession of this unfortunate beast over that time. As you know, white Christian Serbians are among the most intelligent and scientific people in world history. I have no doubt that the wolf was a product of genetic engineering, and that it was programmed to obey commands and carry out certain functions. It may well have been stolen by the Albanians and then turned over to Lurgan for retraining, we have no way of knowing for sure."

"But---but what about that information in the database---?"

"It was a very clever subterfuge, and Ilija and I learned of it as soon as you opened the file in our system. This is why we came into the office shortly after you closed it. We knew that he would be sending you information he had stolen from the Chinese blackmarketers' database. He had already attempted to blackmail us, demanding that we turn over a classified project we were working on for the Government. When we refused, he told us he would make us regret our decision. My men were moving our research data onto trucks for transport to a storage area when he set the wolf against them."

"This is terrible, just terrible," she cried, thanking one of the two hulking bodyguards in the room with them as he handed her a handkerchief.

"I believe our only chance is to have him bring the animal here so we can capture it and apprehend Steve," Evilenko revealed. "As you know, he has that crooked cop Lucic working with him. I have no doubt that they made each other's acquaintance back in Kosovo. Computer piracy is one of the most lucrative crimes in the world right now. Hackers like Lurgan can make millions of dollars buying and selling spyware and virus software. With that kind of money to be made, it takes no great stretch of the imagination to see why Lurgan would go to such extremes to achieve his objectives."

"I was wondering what he was doing with a panel truck," she sobbed. "Lucic said that he had been injured and was on crutches, but I did not once see him getting in or out of the truck. It would make sense that they would make up that story in order to transport that monster dog. He probably stayed inside the truck so the beast did not make noise. When he was outside the facility waiting for me when I escaped from the beast, I should have suspected something. Only I was so terrified, I could only be thankful that he was helping me escape. He brought me straight back to the apartment and told me he would be waiting outside. Mr. Vlasic, do you think---!"

"Not to worry, my dear. As a matter of fact, my associates have spotted him parked up the block from here. As we speak, my men are---"

"Sir, he's just arrived," another man in a black suit entered the office. "We saw a black Camaro park behind the panel truck before the driver got in with Lucic. One of our men did a drive-by and saw Lurgan on the passenger side."

"Good," Evilenko smiled. "I am sure he will make his move very shortly."

"Aren't you going to call the police?" Jana wondered.

"The FBI has asked that we hold our positions until they can put their plan into action," Evilenko replied. "Apparently Lurgan has his Russian connections closing in on our location. They will expect to catch us unawares and steal the research information I was able to rescue from our headquarters when I escaped. You see, my dear, he was sure that I would have my men make contact with you and bring you here. He figured you would lead him directly to us. Having Lucic convince you that he was standing guard justified him remaining on stakeout in front of your home. Only now we have turned the tables, and when the Russians arrive, the FBI will move in and arrest the lot of them."

"So will we just wait here?" Jana was managing to compose herself.

"Actually, you can be of further service to us if you like," Evilenko replied. "I had a reconnaissance unit move into the research plant after Lurgan and Lucic left. They gathered up the remaining documents before notifying the FBI of Lurgan's attack. They are on their way here but are not familiar with New York traffic. Perhaps you can contact them on the Internet and guide them here."

"That will be fine, sir," Jana agreed, feeling like a James Bond girl in the midst of all the intrigue.

"Sir, you are not going to believe this," Evilenko's lieutenant announced as he got off the cell phone once again. "Lurgan got out of the truck and is walking straight over here."

"Good," Evilenko smiled as Jana's eyes widened with apprehension. "Have someone go downstairs and let him in."

Less than an hour later, Steve Lurgan found himself strapped to a metal table in a makeshift forensics lab with tubes protruding from arteries and veins in his body. He had been captured by the Russian mobsters working with Evilenko and brought straight to the second level basement area of the warehouse complex.

When he pulled up behind the panel truck and got in beside Lucic, he told Darko that he intended to walk over to the warehouse to be captured by Evilenko.

"It's our best shot here," he explained. "If I turn myself in, we'll just wait until sundown, and him and his men are history. If he knocks me off and tries to leave here with Jana, you call in your backup."

"I don't understand what you're trying to accomplish here," Darko insisted. "You want me to wait out here until the sun goes down so you can kill everyone in the building?"

"Reason with me. What do you think went down in Catskill after we left? Don't you think he sent someone in behind us to pick up the pieces? If you want to nail him for killing those kids and selling their organs, you're gonna need tons of evidence. If I can make him think he's got time remaining on the clock, he'll be moving his stuff around. The longer I can hang in there with him, the more time we give him to gather the evidence in one place."

Evilenko correctly assumed that Steve was thinking along those lines, and had him brought to the lower level where Dr. Boza Andela awaited. Andela was one of the most notable neurosurgeons in Serbia who had defected to

Albania during the war and became part of the organ black-market. He had conducted most of the surgeries on the corpses of the kidnapped teens that had been brought to Catskill. He escaped along with Evilenko in the moving van transporting the anthrax bomb they had been developing over the past year.

"Dr. Andela will be keeping watch over you while your girlfriend guides our Al Qaeda associates to this location," Evilenko enjoyed the look of astonishment on Steve's face. "They arrived in Montreal a couple of days ago to take possession of the weapon. Their plan was---is---to detonate it near the reservoir in Central Park. Your brutish attempts to force my hand have accelerated our schedule somewhat, but it's better sooner than never."

"You sick bastard!" Steve hissed. "Do you know how many thousands of people you're going to poison?"

"Nothing in life is free, of course," Evilenko replied, adjusting his $100 gold necktie that offset his $500 white silk shirt. "Dr. Andela is already a very wealthy man, as am I and the rest of our team. Al Qaeda's supporters have contributed ten million dollars as payment for the bomb. This, along with the insurance claim for the research lab we will say that you destroyed, as well as the spare body parts and organs we salvaged, will allow us all to walk away well ahead of the game."

"You know Lucic's just waiting to hit the dial button and have the cops swarming this place," Steve strained against his bonds.

"If he was going to do it, he would have done it by now," Evilenko smiled, producing a Glock-17 from a shoulder holster beneath his $5,000 designer suit. "He is hoping to get revenge for his partner getting killed, we both know that. Why else would we think he has been pissing in a can since yesterday? He expects you to turn into the werewolf and kill everyone, rescue that stupid girl, and live happily ever after. Unfortunately I have other plans."

"I hope they include screwing yourself, you son of a bitch!" Steve hissed.

"You do remember these," Evilenko released the ammo clip and popped one of the silver-coated bullets. "It was what you used to put the last poor soul out of his misery. Dr. Andela will be taking a number of tests for the next few hours until sundown. We'll be taking blood, bone marrow, spinal fluid, whatever may be of use. Once you begin experiencing your lycanthropic hallucinations, Dr. Andela will end your suffering permanently."

"Captain Evilenko, I told you before, I am a doctor, not a killer," Andela pleaded. "I have gone back on my Hippocratic Oath more times than I can remember throughout this project, but this is where I draw the line. I will not kill a man, sir, I will not!"

"Calm down, my friend," Evilenko reassured him. "I myself will return here before sundown and handle this myself once your tests are completed. My only concern is that I will have to give full priority to the transfer of the bomb once the Al Qaeda agents arrive. If I am preoccupied, then you will have to attend to this fellow. Rest assured, if he has a manic episode, you may well be faced with the choice of terminating him in your own self-defense."

"I understand what you are telling me, Captain."

"Very good. Carry on."

Darko Lucic sat in the truck as the day wore on, wondering what was going on inside the quiet warehouse on the deserted street. His spine was contracting in agonizing pain on a regular basis, and he had to dump the piss from his can out the window every couple of hours. He was distracted by the thought of having aggravated his spinal injury to cause irreversible damage, but he was certain he could not make it any worse than it was right now.

He watched noon pass by, then the hours dragged past three PM. As it approached five-thirty, he noticed the sun beginning to set in the west and the silhouette of the moon just becoming visible in the azure sky as it became a shade darker. He pulled up his travel bag and pulled out his shoulder holster, grunting as he removed his jacket to strap it on. He then endured the torture of bending forward to buckle on his ankle holster. Finally he reached behind him and pulled out the steel crutches. It would take everything he had to walk into that warehouse, but he had gone too far to turn back now.

He revved up the engine and cruised down the block to the warehouse from where he was parked along a cul-de-sac. He threw open the door and propped up the crutches to brace himself, then slid from the driver's seat and nearly blacked out in transferring his weight to the ground.

"Hey, you fuggin' cop," one of the four Russians at the warehouse entrance challenged him. "This is private property. You're blocking traffic."

"Okay, you bastards get up against the wall, you're all under arrest," Lucic dug his badge out of his pants pocket and stuck it in his breast pocket.

"Get off the property, you fuggin' cripple!" one of the Russians mocked him before they began drawing their pistols.

Just as both sides began opening fire, the sound of a truck engine began growling from the garage area of the warehouse as Bojan Evilenko prepared to meet the Al Qaeda agents at the rendezvous where he would deliver the anthrax bomb. He sent one of his lieutenants up to ensure that Jana Dragana had confirmed the rendezvous with the terrorists near the Watchtower complex by the Brooklyn Bridge. Once that was verified, he would shoot Jana in the head to make sure she had no tales to tell of what she had seen.

The lieutenant heard the gunfire outside and rushed to the aid of his comrades, putting Jana out of his mind for the moment. Jana, hearing the shots ringing out from the street below, rushed to the window and could see Lucic taking shelter behind a street lamppost as he exchanged fire with the Russians. She pulled out her cell phone and found that not only was her battery running low, but she could not get a signal. She began weeping as she watched the gunfight below, having no idea of what might happen to her.

Dr. Andela also heard the gunfire and stared frantically at the door, expecting the footsteps of Bojan Evilenko to no avail. At once he saw Steve's eyes roll back into his head, and his back arched hideously before he started convulsing. Andela stared at the Glock on the table alongside his medical equipment which he had used to draw fluids and samples from Steve throughout the day. Yet he was not about to shoot a man, much less in cold blood. He had sold his soul to Evilenko for over a million dollars in a Swiss bank account, but here he would draw the line.

He could not believe his eyes as he watched Steve's ribcage expand, swelling to almost twice its normal size. His hair and nail growth accelerated freakishly, and his limbs began twisting as tree branches into terrible deformations. His face was contorted by pain, yet it appeared that the unnatural growth of his hair and nails had spread to his teeth as they began jutting from his lips. Steve then let out a terrible scream, one almost identical to that which he heard at a killing field near Kosovo where Albanian Muslims had gunned down thirty Serbian Christian civilians. Only this was not the screams of terrified women and children. These were the screams of the damned begging for release from the pits of Hell.

It was almost as if watching someone shaving, or seeing something burn in a fire. The metamorphosis was so sudden and absolute that when he focused on one area of the body, another was transforming at an astounding rate. When Andela tore his eyes away from Steve's tortured face, he saw that his entire body was matted with hair and that his legs had curled into massive balls of steely muscle ending in stick-like shins and claw-like clubbed feet. Something that looked almost like a tail was protruding from beneath his buttocks. When he looked back up at Steve's face, his nose and jaw was beginning to protrude as a Neandertal.

The screaming had given way to an unearthly roar that chilled the marrow in Andela's bones. It was the roar of neither man nor beast, rather that of the Devil himself. Andela fell back in stark terror, and at once the beast that was Steve Lurgan snapped its bonds as if it was toilet paper. The Doctor nearly swooned as the monster stood on the table, towering over him as the fanged jaws gaped as those of a killer shark. He stared into its eyes, which glowed as embers as it stared into Andela's soul. The Doctor began weeping hysterically, and he lost control of his bowels as a foul stench filled the room. Once again the sound of gunfire could be heard outside, and at once the giant wolf jumped off the table and through the door as if made of balsa wood.

Outside, Darko was huddled behind the lamppost for dear life as multiple shots had punched their way into the metal but had yet to penetrate both sides. He fired single shots in response, holding off the four gunmen who were hiding in doorways, trying to draw closer to get a clean shot at Lucic. They cursed and taunted him, hoping he would make a break for the truck so they could shoot him in the back. They knew that Evilenko was getting ready to pull up the steel door of the garage and drive off with the anthrax bomb, at which point they would have fulfilled their end of their agreement with him.

The gunmen sensed movement behind them, and turned to stare aghast at the giant beast approaching them. It was the kind of terror that would grip one at a zoo, in turning to find out that one of the animals had escaped its cage and had crept up behind them. They swung and began firing at the monster, which sprang at the closest gunman and engulfed his entire face in its jaws. Their eyes bulged as they heard the bones of the man's face crunching under the pressure, blood spurting across the concrete pavement as his body went limp.

Darko took the initiative by hobbling forth on one crutch, somehow balancing himself as he opened fire at his attackers. One of the men buckled as bullets tore into his back, and another wilted from a bullet to the back of his skull. The beast, meanwhile, had jumped the fourth man and snapped his extended shooting arm in half like a breadstick. He fell screaming to the ground as Darko stared into the eyes of the blood-drenched wolf.

"Okay, go easy, Steve," Darko managed, his testicles shriveled with fright. "I know you're in there somewhere. We have to rescue Jana and stop Evilenko. His truck's getting ready to take off, and I'll never get back behind the wheel in time."

At once the giant wolf rushed off in the direction of the garage. Darko looked up and saw Jana looking down from the second floor window, and beckoned her down as he squatted agonizingly to retrieve his other crutch. He only hoped that the cops did not show up, or that a passerby did not hear the screams of the maimed gunman and call the police. He had no doubt that if Evilenko escaped, he would sell the harvested organs to the Chinese before fleeing the country. He had not the slightest idea about the anthrax bomb. His only concern was arresting Evilenko before he could leave the premises. Yet he would not have been surprised if Evilenko had rigged the truck with explosives to destroy the evidence if necessary.

He hobbled agonizedly from the front of the warehouse to the garage, tears of pain streaming down his cheeks. He saw the sliding door had been partially raised, and managed to bend over enough to slip inside. He saw the huge truck idling before him, and to his left Evilenko sat cowering before the beast as it had him trapped by the control panel in the corner.

"Okay, Bojan, just don't make any false moves. That thing just tore up four of your guys outside," Darko inched carefully towards the truck. "It's all over, we don't want anyone else to get killed here. I'm gonna try and make it to the truck and turn it off. Whatever you do, don't get that damned thing excited."

"It's Lurgan, you know that, you fool," Evilenko replied hoarsely. "He still can think clearly and understand, otherwise I'd be dead. I've already armed the bomb, it's set to go off within the hour. By the time you call your friends and they send the bomb squad, the weapon will have covered all of Flatbush with anthrax."

"What bomb?" Lucic demanded.

"We have successfully completed development of an anthrax bomb for an Al Qaeda cell here in North America," Evilenko managed a chortle. "In the event our deal with the

Chinese was cancelled or sabotaged by the likes of you, we made alternative plans to sell the bomb to Al Qaeda before fleeing the country. One of the features we installed was an irreversible manual detonator in case we were trapped or captured as we are now. It has little value but to provide us with a measure of revenge against those who have foiled our plans."

At once, Jana Dragana slipped under the overhead door and nearly swooned at the sight of the beast just a few feet away from her.

"Jana!" Darko called to her. "Don't worry, everything's okay, just don't make any sudden moves. This crazy son of a bitch set off an anthrax bomb in that truck. I don't the bomb squad can get here in time to stop it!"

At once the beast turned and stared into Darko's eyes, and he fought the quivering in his chest as he tried to focus on a sudden impulse in his brain.

"The underground vault," he realized. "If we can get this damned thing inside the vault on Staten Island, it may be able to contain the blast!"

The giant wolf froze Evilenko in place with its guttural snarls as Darko hobbled around to the back of the truck with Jana behind him. She helped him open the door and they stood in awe of the black cylindrical device that appeared about ten feet in diameter. It had a large round device on top of it, and resembled a flying saucer from the movies.

"How are we going to move it? It must weigh a ton!" Jana was dismayed.

"We'll worry about that when we get there. Get in the truck."

They watched in fascination as the giant wolf sank its teeth around Evilenko's waistline, grabbing his belt and the front of his pants. The Captain cried out in alarm as the monster's teeth tore his skin in the process. It prodded and shoved him backward towards the rear of the truck, finally releasing him as they reached the back door. Evilenko instinctively rolled into the vehicle, and the beast jumped in on the other side of the bomb as Darko shut the door behind them. He hobbled back around to the control panel to the overhead door, trying to fight the blinding pain as he raised it all the way. He then made it back to the cab and drove the truck out of the garage towards the Verrazano-Narrows Bridge to Staten Island.

It took nearly a half hour to reach the mansion, and Darko knew they were in a race against time. The truck remained silent throughout the drive as Darko was fighting to keep from slumping over in agony while Jana stared out the window in distraction. Evilenko tried once or twice to speak to the wolf, but its horrible growls clutched everyone's heart with terror. They finally pulled into the driveway, and Darko managed to lower himself to the pavement. Jana saw the agony he was in, and rushed over to help him down.

Darko opened the garage door and drove the truck in, and he was exhilarated to find that there was a freight elevator installed by the drug dealers allowing them to transport bulky items to the underground area. He opened the door to let Evilenko and the beast out. Evilenko jumped aside as the monster set its jaws around one of the spaces cut into both sides of the ridge of the device. It hauled the bomb out of the truck so that the device landed on the garage floor with a deafening crash. Darko guessed that it must have weighed over three hundred pounds, which gave them an inkling of the power of the creature.

It next pushed the bomb into the elevator with its front paws, and Darko would remember how funny that might have been had they not been frightened out of their wits. He had not even bothered to pull his pistol out again as Evilenko would not have dreamed of running from this thing. Once it had loaded the bomb into the car, it growled menacingly at Evilenko, the gory entrails of his victims still caked on its muzzle and chest. Evilenko instinctively stepped into the elevator, staring at the control panel as a last possible means of escape.

"Don't even think of it," Darko said as he and Jana stepped in behind him, followed by the wolf. "No matter where you go, this thing will find you."

The elevator hummed as its doors closed and it slowly descended to the underground chambers. When they reopened, the wolf began shoving the bomb out towards the vault where it had been trapped just the night before. Darko hobbled over and entered the code, and the vault door slowly swung open. They watched in apprehension as the beast pushed the bomb into the vault, then used its muzzle to slam the steel door shut. It then walked over and laid down in front of the elevator door. The three of them looked at each other, realizing they had no choice but to wait here until the bomb went off.

About ten minutes later, the three of them nearly jumped out of their skins as an explosion the like of they never heard went off in the vault. Despite the fact that the bomb was locked in the vault, the roar was so great that the plaster cracked along the ceilings and floors throughout the basement. Items were thrown from shelves, and the monitor of the surveillance system exploded as it popped from the console and fell to the concrete. They could hear the burglar alarms going off throughout the house and realized the police would be on the way.

With that, the wolf rose from the concrete and padded

over to the vault door. It rose on its hind legs and hit the red emergency button on the control panel with its muzzle, causing the door to open.

"Steve! No!" Darko yelled, causing Jana to stare at him in wonderment.

The wolf paid no heed, snarling and growling at Evilenko, hunching its massive shoulders as if ready to pounce. The Captain's eyes darted about wildly, looking for a way to elude the monster. As he moved an inch in any direction, the beast shifted as if to cut him off and leap at him. The creature's snarls and roars were so terrific that Evilenko slipped inside the vault in a desperate effort to escape. With that, the wolf rose and slammed the door behind him.

"Steve! You can't---!" Darko gasped, but at once the wolf became as a shepherd dog, snarling and encircling them to force them back into the elevator. They numbly did as it bade them, and finally the monster stepped in alongside them. Darko hit the control panel to bring them back to the grade level, the screams and cries of Bojan Evilenko echoing in their ears.

CHAPTER TEN

Dear Steve,

By the time you read this I will be far away from New York, far from the terrible memories of my recent experiences. Unfortunately it will also put me far away from you, and I guess it is how it must be.

The man I knew as Zora Vlasic told me many lies, and truths mixed with lies. I have read the papers and I now know who he really is and all the horrible things he has done. The only thing that went unexplained was the wolf that killed all those people. They said it was under investigation and that they feared it would be a trend that had to be stopped. All I can say is that I hope you are not implicated.

I can no longer ignore the fact that I am the only person who has been involved with all three of these incidents. The police are fully aware of it, but your friend Darko has cleared me of suspicion. He has distracted them to look elsewhere, and I take the advantage to leave New York for good. I have no doubt that if I stay, one day that wolf will reappear in my life. That is something I never wish to experience again.

You are a wonderful man with a great personality, and I will always cherish the times we shared together, and the time I considered you my best friend. Only the last chapter I will try and blot from my mind, though I believe it will be a nightmare I will always live with.

God bless you, Steve, You will be in my heart always.

Love, Jana

"Well, I guess that's it," Steve exhaled tautly as Darko set the letter down on the coffee table between them in his living room. "That was my only reason for living."

"Come on, Steve," Darko chided him gently. "Even though you didn't get any credit for it, you and I know what you did. Evilenko's blackmarketing ring was smashed, his Al Qaeda connections got picked up and his Chinese connections are on the run. The FBI invaded his plant in the Catskills and had a field day with his computer databases.

There was enough evidence to put everyone in his crew away for life, plus they got Andela to turn State's witness. You're the one who should've gotten all the medals, not me. As a matter of fact, I want to give them to you. I insist."

"There's only one last thing you can do for me," Steve replied quietly. He wordlessly produced a Glock-17, with a clip they both knew was loaded with silver-coated bullets.

"No fuggin' way, Steve," he held up his hands. "No fuggin' way. I'm a cop, not an executioner. You want mercy killing, I can give you dozens of names."

"Try this on for size," Lurgan replied, putting the gun down on the table. "If you took this thing from me, it'd get you out of that wheelchair permanently. If you moved out to the desert, somewhere like Arizona or New Mexico, even California, you'd still be drawing your disability, you wouldn't need to work. All you'd have to do is let this thing out into the desert once a month for a few days, during the full moon cycle. At first it takes getting used to, but after a while you start remembering things, and you take control."

"Don't even tell me you had control over that thing."

"Not like that," Steve insisted. "Look, it's a wolf, you saw it. It acts on instinct, yet it has the human factor in its subconscious, we saw that. It can be benevolent at times. You just have to put it where it's not exposed to violence or it's not attacked. It will even flee if it has the chance."

"Look, you sound like you're trying to get me to adopt a dog, and you've got it in your head that if I shoot you with a silver bullet, all sales are final," Darko scoffed. "Forget about it. Hey, take it to the media, give *Good Morning America* an exclusive. The Government won't be able to touch you then. They'll put you in a private facility where you'd be free to come and go, and you'd just have to check in during the cycle for observation and confinement. Killing yourself is bullshit, Steve. I'm not comfortable with that thing sitting up on the table. Put it away."

"It's over for me, Darko," Steve picked it up slowly. "Jana was all I really had to live for. I can't spend the rest of my life looking after this wolf."

"Steve! No!" Darko yelled as Steve put the gun to his head and pulled the trigger.

At once it was as if a torrent of ectoplasm emerged from Steve's mouth, the ghosts of dozens of tortured beings spewing in an arc over the coffee table and plunging as a phantasmal dagger into Darko's heart. Lucic's eyes rolled up in his head and he began convulsing with such violence that he fell from his wheelchair as if dead on the floor.

He did not move again until a half hour later when the police arrived.

It was about a year later when Jana Dragana was admiring the sunset from the enormous glass window overlooking the mountainside from her luxurious home near the Sonora Desert in Arizona. The sun crackled in fiery resignation, splotching the skies with orange and gold as the cobalt darkness engulfed the horizon.

"About ready to go?" she asked quietly.

"Yeah, it's about that time," Darko Lucic replied, dressed only in his terrycloth robe and slippers as he headed for their workout room in the spacious ranch house. "We'll take a ride out to California when I get back."

"Love you."

"Love you too," he said as he closed the door to the gym softly behind him.

She went to the kitchen and absently began rinsing the dishes from dinner, gazing out at the landscape. New York was a distant memory from another past, and all her addictions and cares were left far behind. There was only one memory that remained with her, and she had finally come to terms with it as best as she ever would.

There was a movement outside off towards the east wing of the house, and she stepped away from the kitchen counter and looked out the sliding glass door. There she saw the giant wolf as it walked around the house, staring into her eyes.

It then turned away and padded off into the sunset once more.

Dear reader,

We hope you enjoyed reading *Wolf Man*. Please take a moment to leave a review, even if it's a short one. Your opinion is important to us.

Discover more books by John Reinhard Dizon at

https://www.nextchapter.pub/authors/john-reinhard-dizon

Want to know when one of our books is free or discounted? Join the newsletter at

http://eepurl.com/bqqB3H

Best regards,

John Reinhard Dizon and the Next Chapter Team

NOTES

Chapter 2

1. New World Order

Chapter 4

1. Chinese Secret Service
2. Voodoo priest

Chapter 6

1. Mob soldiers

CPSIA information can be obtained
at www.ICGtesting.com
Printed in the USA
BVHW041527180121
598054BV00016B/491/J